D0980789

ST. MARTIN'S PAPERBACKS TITLES
BY MATT BRAUN

BLACK FOX
OUTLAW KINGDOM
LORDS OF THE LAND
CIMARRON JORDAN
BLOODY HAND
NOBLE OUTLAW
TEXAS EMPIRE
THE SAVAGE LAND
RIO HONDO
THE GAMBLERS
DOC HOLLIDAY
YOU KNOW MY NAME
THE BRANNOCKS
THE LAST STAND
RIO GRANDE
GENTLEMAN ROGUE
THE KINCAIDS
EL PASO
INDIAN TERRITORY
BLOODSPORT
SHADOW KILLERS
BUCK COLTER
KINCH RILEY
DEATHWALK
HICKOK & CODY
THE WILD ONES
HANGMAN'S CREEK
JURY OF SIX
THE SPOILERS
MANHUNTER
THE WARLORDS

DEADWOOD

Matt Braun

St. Martin's Paperbacks

Published by arrangement with Pocket Books.

DEADWOOD

ISBN: 0-312-98180-5

Printed in the United States of America

Pocket Books edition / December 1981
St. Martin's Paperbacks edition / August 2003

St. Martin's Paperbacks are published by St. Martin's Press, 175 Fifth Avenue, New York, NY 10010.

10 9 8 7 6 5 4 3 2 1

TO
MY FOLKS
ON THEIR
GOLDEN WEDDING
ANNIVERSARY

Author's Note

Deadwood was one of the richest gold camps in the Old West. The lure of overnight wealth proved a lodestone for prospectors and miners, grifters and outlaws, and a wide assortment of characters who inhabited the vice district. Vast amounts of money exchanged hands, and as a result, violence was commonplace. The town was tough and dangerous, no place for the faint of heart. Only the strong survived in Deadwood.

Yet the untold story had nothing to do with gold. Until now a footnote to history, it was the politics of Dakota Territory that deserved the greater infamy. Corruption and graft were rampant, and the stakes far exceeded the transitory riches of a mining camp. Power brokers and the vested interests, during the early 1880s, were involved in a systematic looting of the territory itself. The chief conspirator was the governor, and few public officials were untouched by the web of intrigue and shady practices. Dakota Territory was a textbook example of the system gone wrong, and the ultimate price was staggering. Ambition proved the deadliest killer of all.

Deadwood is for the most part a true account. Some license has been taken with time and date and place. The historical characters, however, are represented as they actually were, with no apology and no attempt at whitewash. Within the framework of the story, Butch Cassidy and Hole-in-the-Wall are also depicted with true-to-life authenticity. The tall tales surrounding Hole-in-the-Wall, like so many Old West myths, were fostered by outlaws and widely exaggerated by the press. On the other hand, the lawmen central to the story required no literary invention. Nat Boswell and Seth Bullock *were* legend in their own time.

Luke Starbuck represents yet another breed of lawman. A detective and an undercover operative, he was a master of disguise. His fame as a manhunter was unsurpassed, and his reputation as a mankiller was known throughout the Old West. His assignment in *Deadwood* deals more with truth than fiction. What he unearths during the course of his investigation is based on documented fact. He saw it happen exactly the way it's told.

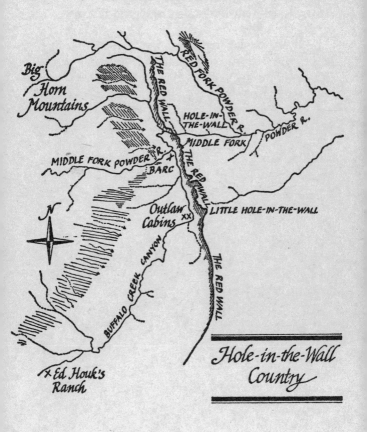

Hole-in-the-Wall
Country

DEADWOOD

Chapter One

Starbuck checked the loads in his old Colt. Then he lowered the hammer on an empty chamber and stuffed the sixgun into a crossdraw holster. His suit jacket concealed the rig with no telltale bulge.

On the way out the door, he jammed a Stetson on his head and paused to inspect himself in the foyer mirror. His suit was conservative, as befitted a man in his profession, and he wore a four-in-hand tie that was equally sober. His appointment today at the Denver Club required that he look the part, create a certain impression. He thought he would pass muster.

In the hallway, he bypassed the newly installed elevator. His suite in the Brown Palace was located on the top floor, but he still preferred the stairs. Along with a daily regimen of exercise, the hike up and down four flights of stairs kept him in reasonable shape. He emerged into the lobby some minutes later and walked directly to the street door. Outside, he turned uptown beneath a warm noonday sun.

Springtime was to Starbuck the best of all seasons. Off in the distance, the Rockies were still blanketed with snow, towering skyward into the clouds. Yet by late May the city itself was slowly recovering from the onslaughts of winter. The air was clear and exhilarating, and with the mud season at an end, the streets were baked hard as stone. Passersby seemed somehow uplifted in spirit, and even the clang of trolley cars took on a merry ring. Starbuck's mood was no less buoyant. The weather, combined with one of his swift-felt hunches, gave him a sense of promise. It looked to be a good day.

Once through the business district, Starbuck continued along Larimer Street. His immediate destination was the Tenderloin. There, within a few square blocks, every vice known to man was available for a price. Saloons and gaming dives catered to the sporting crowd, and variety theaters featured headline acts from the vaudeville circuit. The racy blend of fun and games attracted high rollers from all across the West.

One block over, on Holladay Street, was Denver's infamous red-light district. Known locally as the Row, it was a lusty fleshpot, with a veritable crush of dollar cribs. Girls waited in doorways, soliciting customers, available by the trick or by the hour. Yet, while these hook shops dominated, there was no scarcity of parlor houses on the Row. Essentially a high-class bagnio, the parlor house offered younger girls and a greater variety, all at steeper prices. Something over a thousand soiled doves plied their trade on Holladay Street, and each in her own way was a civic benefactress. The revenues generated by their license fees were the only thing that kept the city treasury afloat.

For those with a taste for the bizarre, there was Hop Alley. A narrow passageway running between Larimer and Holladay, it was Denver's version of Lotus Land. Chinese fan-tan parlors vied with the faint, sweet odor of opium dens, and those addicted to the Orient's heady delights beat a steady path to this back-street world of pipe dreams. To a select clientele, young China dolls were for sale as well.

Still, it was not gambling or girls that brought Starbuck to the Tenderloin. Whenever he was in town, he made a practice of dropping by Murphy's Exchange, otherwise known as the Slaughterhouse. A watering hole for the underworld, it was home away from home to thimbleriggers, bunco artists, and a wide assortment of shady characters. Moreover, it was the chief source of gossip, not to mention a message drop, for those who lived on the fringes of the law. To a private detective, that made it a lode of hard intelligence. One to be mined at regular intervals.

Starbuck was known to those who frequented Murphy's Exchange. His reputation as a manhunter—some called him a mankiller—was widely celebrated throughout the West. Only last month he had been instrumental in the death of Jesse James, and previous cases had pitted him against such notorious gunmen as Wyatt Earp and Billy the Kid. Over the years he'd been retained by banks and train companies, and he was reputed to have killed at least twenty outlaws. Yet, for all his renown with a gun, it was his skill as a detective that kept his services in constant demand. He always got results, and it was no secret that he enjoyed his work. He was a hunter of men who seemed born to the job.

Upon entering the saloon, Starbuck walked to a vacant spot at the end of the bar. The noontime crowd, after a quick glance in his direction, suddenly got busy minding their own business. Apart from his reputation with a gun, he was also noted as a man who brooked no familiarity. A strapping six-footer, he was lean and tough, full-spanned through the shoulders. His features were ruggedly forceful, with a square jaw and wide brow, and a thatch of light chestnut hair. But it was his eyes—smoky blue and impersonal—that gave other men pause. His gaze was detached, not so much cold as stoic. A look of one who makes alliances but not friends. The look of a loner, and someone best left alone.

Jack Murphy, the proprietor, moved forward to greet him. Their relationship was one of quid pro quo—a favor here for a favor there—and it had proved mutually profitable in the past. A squat fat man, with a greasy moonlike face and a larcenous disposition, Murphy had only one redeeming quality. He was Starbuck's principal informant in the Denver underworld.

"Afternoon, Luke." Murphy wiped the counter with a dirty bar rag. "Buy you a drink?"

Starbuck wagged his head. "Guess I'll pass."

"What can I do for you, then?"

"Wondered what you've heard on the grapevine."

"Nothing special." Murphy stared back at him with round, guileless eyes. "Things are pretty quiet."

"Things are never that quiet," Starbuck said pointedly. "Try me and see."

"Well, lemme think." Murphy furrowed his brow. "Couple of weeks ago Frank Loving got it down in Trinidad. A saloonkeeper by the name of Allen put his lights out."

"Cockeyed Frank Loving?" Starbuck inquired. "The gambler?"

"Some folks said it wasn't gambling, not the way he dealt."

"Anything else?"

"You remember Jim Courtright?" When Starbuck

nodded, he went on. "A pair of toughnuts tried to rob an ore shipment he was guarding. He shot 'em deader'n hell."

"Whereabouts?"

"New Mexico Territory."

"Nothing closer to home?"

"Like I said," Murphy reminded him, "things are slow."

Starbuck gave him a stony look. "I don't suppose you've heard anything about William Dexter, the lawyer?"

"Not a peep." Murphy fidgeted uncomfortably. "Why do you ask?"

"I've got my reasons."

"Take some advice, Luke." Murphy cleared his throat, leaned closer. "Don't get crosswise of Dexter. He runs with the uptown crowd, and they play rough."

"Yeah?" Starbuck's eyebrows narrowed in a quick characteristic squint of mockery. "I always heard that bunch prided themselves on being upstanding Christians."

"That's what I mean!" Murphy grunted. "God's on their side—leastways to hear them tell it—and that makes them double-damn dangerous."

"I'll keep it in mind." Starbuck consulted his pocket watch. "Guess I'd better move along, Jack. Wouldn't do to be late for an appointment."

"Hope to hell it's not with Dexter!"

"You really don't want to know . . . do you?"

"Not me!" Murphy's lips peeled back in a weak smile. "I just got a sudden case of deaf."

Starbuck flipped him a salute. "See you around."

"Take care, Luke."

"I always do."

Outside, Starbuck turned from the Tenderloin and headed back uptown. He thought to himself the saloonkeeper's advice was worth the trip. He would indeed take care.

The Denver Club was the sanctum sanctorum of the city's upper crust. Only recently constructed, it was an imposing stone building, four stories high and occupying nearly half a block. Like some medieval fortress, it commanded the intersection of Seventeenth Street and Glenarm.

Crossing the street, Starbuck was reminded that the club was a symbol of Denver's power structure. Membership was restricted to those of wealth and position, the elite of the business world. Gentlemen met there to socialize and discuss deals, and the pacts they struck often produced a ripple effect throughout the whole of Colorado. Their numbers included bankers and merchant princes, railroad barons and mine owners, financiers and lawyers. As a group, their influence was incalculable, and their political connections extended to the state house itself. They were, in every sense of the word, the aristocracy of Denver's social order.

For his part, Starbuck held the power brokers in mild contempt. His own origins were humble; but like many of Denver's upper class, he too was a self-made man. A cowhand turned range detective, he'd grown and prospered, slowly developing a reputation as the leading private investigator in the West. His investment portfolio—which included municipal bonds, real estate, and various mining stocks—now exceeded a quarter million dollars. Yet success and personal wealth had not gone to his head. At bottom, he was still a man of simple tastes, no sophisticate. Nor was he under any great compulsion to curry favor with those who ruled Denver. His opinion of himself was what counted, nothing more.

A similar attitude extended to his professional life. He worked by choice—rather than necessity—for the simplest of reasons. He took pride in his craft, and derived a certain emotional sustenance from danger. High stakes were the lodestone, and in his view, a manhunt was the ultimate wager. Financal independence, of course, allowed him to pick and choose from the many assignments offered. He accepted a case because of the degree of risk entailed, the challenge. To win, there must exist a chance to lose. And each time out, he bet his life.

The interior of the Denver Club was scarcely less than Starbuck had expected. The ceilings were high, and the staircase facing the entrance rose upward like an aerial corridor. Dark paneling predominated, with a massive chandelier suspended overhead and lush Persian carpet underfoot. An attendant escorted him into a room immediately off the central hallway. The decor was opulent, with velvet drapes and damask wallpaper, all heightened by a black marble fireplace and luxuriant leather furniture. An immense oil painting of the Colorado Rockies hung resplendent over the fireplace.

A man in his late forties turned from a sunlit window. He was attired in a black broadcloth coat and gray-striped trousers, with a pearl stickpin nestled in an elegant silk cravat. His voice was well modulated and his manners impeccable. He walked forward, extending his hand.

"How nice of you to come, Mr. Starbuck."

"Pleasure's all mine, Mr. Dexter."

"Won't you have a seat?" Dexter let go of his hand, motioned him into the room. "May I offer you something to drink?"

"No, thanks." Starbuck settled into an overstuffed chair. "I never mix liquor with business."

"An admirable trait." Dexter dismissed the attendant with a faint nod. He took a chair opposite Starbuck and crossed his legs. "I do appreciate your promptness, Mr. Starbuck."

"Your note indicated it was a matter of some urgency."

"And so it is."

William Dexter, like everyone else in Denver, was aware of Starbuck's reputation. He knew the detective was admired for his cool judgment and nervy quickness in tight situations. So now, assessing the man and the moment, he wasted no time on preliminaries. He went straight to the point.

"I asked you here on behalf of a client, Mr. Starbuck. I have been empowered to offer you a . . . commission."

"Commission." Starbuck repeated the word without inflection. "Would you care to spell that out?"

"Of course," Dexter replied genially. "My client owns a rather substantial copper mine in Butte, Montana. Day before yesterday, the paymaster was brutally beaten and robbed. My client wants the payroll returned."

"How much money's involved?"

"Forty-seven hundred dollars."

"Hardly seems worth the effort."

"On the contrary," Dexter said with exaggerated

gravity. "My client is willing to pay you five thousand dollars now and five thousand dollars upon completion."

Starbuck's mouth curled in a sardonic smile. "Why do I get the impression we just stopped talking about the payroll?"

"Very discerning, Mr. Starbuck." Dexter examined him with a kind of bemused curiosity. "Actually, my client's principal concern is justice. He wants an object lesson made of the robber. A warning, as it were, to anyone with similar ideas."

The message was familiar. Couched in discreet terms, it was one Starbuck had heard many times before. He was being asked to dispense summary justice, kill an outlaw. His expression revealed nothing.

"Why not let the law handle it?"

Dexter slowly shook his head. "I regret to say that avenue has been foreclosed. The sheriff in Butte identified the robber—a ruffian by the name of Mike Cassidy—but he declined to carry it further. Valor, it seems, has its limits."

Starbuck studied him with a thoughtful frown. "Are you saying the sheriff lost his nerve?"

"I am indeed!" Dexter announced. "Not without reason, however. Perhaps you've heard of a place called Hole-in-the-Wall?"

There was a long silence. Hole-in-the-Wall, located in the wilds of Wyoming, was considered an inaccessible outlaw sanctuary. To Starbuck's knowledge, no lawman had ever ventured into the remote mountain fastness and returned alive. The assignment, until now a seemingly mundane affair, suddenly piqued his interest. At length, his tone matter-of-fact, he nodded.

"Let's say I've heard of it. So what?"

"Quite simply," Dexter observed, "the robber has taken refuge in Hole-in-the-Wall. So far as we can determine, no peace officer will go near the place. We thought you might be the man for the job."

"In other words"—Starbuck kept his gaze level and cool—"you want me to locate Mike Cassidy and kill him. Is that the gist of it?"

"I didn't say that," Dexter remarked stiffly. "Of course, by entering Hole-in-the-Wall, I should imagine you'd have no choice. I understand those desperadoes refuse to be taken alive."

Starbuck regarded him with great calmness. "Who's your client?"

"Ira Lloyd," Dexter informed him. "Owner of the Grubstake Mining Company. And, I hasten to add, one of the wealthiest men in Butte."

"Why use a go-between? Why didn't he contact me himself?"

"For one thing, he rarely travels to Denver. For another, a man in his position prefers anonymity in such matters. All things considered, an intermediary seems very much in order. Don't you agree, Mr. Starbuck?"

A moment elapsed while the two men stared at each other. Then Starbuck's mouth twisted in a gallows grin. "Well, it's tidy, Mr. Dexter. And I do admire tidy arrangements."

"Then you'll take the case?"

Starbuck uncoiled from his chair and stood. "I'll let you know."

"Let me know?" Dexter echoed blankly. "When?"

"When I make up my mind."

Starbuck turned and walked from the room. William Dexter watched him out the door, then eased back in his chair and gazed up at the panoramic painting over the fireplace. A slow, foxy smile creased the corners of his mouth.

Chapter Two

Starbuck walked directly from the Denver Club to his office. The building was around the corner from the Windsor Hotel, centrally located to the business district. His agency, which consisted of a two-room suite, was on the second floor. He seldom went there.

For several years Starbuck's office had been under his hat. During the period he'd worked as a range detective, there had been no need for a permanent location. With time, however, the nature of his business had undergone a gradual change. From chasing horse thieves and cattle rustlers, it had slowly evolved into investigative work of greater complexity. Wells Fargo was his first major client, and within a span of three years his reputation rivaled that of the Pinkertons. By 1882, he was regarded as the foremost detective west of the Mississippi. His list of clients read like a directory of railroads, banks, and stagecoach lines.

Upon locating in Denver, he had established a modest office. A one-room cubbyhole, and quite spartan by normal standards, it had served as a clearinghouse for correspondence. Since he was usually off on a case, there was need for little more than a secretary and an address. Only recently had he decided to expand his headquarters. An adjoining room had been leased, and he'd had a connecting door installed. A desk and a chair gave it some semblance of a private office, but he used it for an altogether different purpose. There, locked in a massive safe, he maintained a repository of hard intelligence on the criminal element. It was, in effect, a rogues' gallery of western outlaws.

Upstairs, Starbuck entered the office and pegged his Stetson on a hat rack. Verna Phelps, his secretary, glanced up from an accounting ledger. She was a spinster, on the sundown side of thirty, and prim as a missionary. She wore her hair in a tight chignon, and pince-nez eyeglasses were clipped onto the end of her nose. She looked every inch the old maid.

"Good afternoon." She greeted him with starch civility. "How was your meeting?"

"I haven't decided yet."

"Pardon me?"

"It's a queer setup," Starbuck told her. "Dexter's only the front man. Turns out he's representing some mine owner up in Butte."

Verna lifted an eyebrow in question. "Why should that bother you?"

"Don't know," Starbuck admitted. "Guess I get a little leery when a man won't do business face to face."

"Some people would consider it routine practice. After all, a lawyer often has power of attorney to act in his client's behalf."

"Maybe." Starbuck hesitated, then shrugged. "Or maybe it's Dexter that worries me. I never did trust a man who's got nothing to hide. And he comes across like every word's sworn testimony."

"Humph!" Verna sniffed and looked away. "Your cynicism never ceases to amaze me."

Starbuck grinned. "So far, it's kept me fogging a mirror. Which isn't exactly no small feat, considering the company I keep."

Verna Phelps conceded the point. She appreciated the danger involved in Starbuck's work, and understood the need for expedient methods. She even took a certain macabre pride in the number of men he'd killed. Yet she thought him too cynical for his own good, and secretly worried it would lead to some darker alienation of the spirit. She abruptly switched topics.

"Speaking of company," she observed, squinting querulously over her glasses, "Miss Montana sent a street urchin by with a message."

"Urchin?"

"That's correct!" Verna said with frosty disapproval. "No doubt some poor orphan she and her associates have corrupted with handouts."

"The girls at the Alcazar would be mighty pleased to know you've elevated them to 'associates.' "

"A charitable term," Verna noted with a feisty scowl. "Would you care to hear my real opinion?"

"I'd sooner not." Starbuck warded her off with upraised palms. "Let's just stick to the message."

"Miss Montana," Verna said sharply, "requests the pleasure of your company at tonight's performance. I have the distinct impression she feels you've been neglecting her."

Starbuck's expression was one of amiable tolerance. "What do you think, Verna? Should I give her a break or not?"

"I'm sure I don't care one way or the other."

By no means monogamous, Starbuck entertained any number of women in his hotel suite. Yet his affair with Lola Montana—a headliner at the Alcazar Variety Theater—appeared to be a thing of some permanence. Her disclaimer aside, Verna had mixed emotions on that score. She applauded his constancy to one woman, which was a singular departure from his normal behavior. Still, she thought the woman— who shamelessly flaunted herself onstage—was little more than a common strumpet. It was all very perturbing, and Starbuck himself did nothing to alleviate her anxiety. His overall attitude was that of a boar grizzly in rutting season. He took his women where he found them.

Verna considered it not only scandalous, but thoroughly reprehensible. And more than a little titillating. She often wondered how Lola Montana felt, locked naked in the intimacy of Starbuck's embrace. The mere thought prompted a vicarious sensation that gave her naughty dreams, and vivid awakenings. Even now, she felt a tingling warmth along her loins, and her face suddenly reddened to the hairline. She took hold of herself, ruthlessly purged the thought.

"You have your message," she said in a waspish tone. "Now, perhaps we can return to business. You were telling me about Mr. Dexter."

"Nothing more to tell," Starbuck said equably. "He just struck me as a man with secrets . . . lots of secrets."

"Then you intend to refuse the case?"

"Nooo," Starbuck said slowly. "Tell you the truth, I'm tempted to have a crack at it."

"Oh?" Verna gave him a quizzical glance. "Something unusual?"

"Out of the ordinary," Starbuck affirmed. "He wants me to track down a payroll robber—last reported at Hole-in-the-Wall."

"Hole-in-the-Wall!" Verna suddenly appeared apprehensive. "I understood Hole-in-the-Wall was certain death to lawmen!"

"Yeah." Starbuck chuckled, and lowered one eyelid in a conspiratorial wink. "A place where angels fear to tread. Sounds like just my speed, doesn't it?"

"It sounds like you could get yourself killed."

"What the hell!" Starbuck deadpanned. "Nobody lives forever."

"On the other hand," Verna said, a hint of reproach in her voice, "why leap at a challenge simply because it's there?"

"Always look before I leap," Starbuck noted wryly. "Suppose you dig out your directory on mining companies? I'd like to know if there's a Grubstake Mining Company in Butte."

"Anything else?"

"Dexter told me the owner's name is Ira Lloyd. Check that, too."

Verna rummaged around in the bottom drawer of her desk and pulled out a directory published by the Denver Stock Exchange. Starbuck left her flipping pages and moved into the inner office. He walked to a large double-door safe standing against the far wall. He spun a sequence on the combination lock, then turned the handle and swung open one door. On an inside shelf were stacked four loose-leaf ledgers, each of them bound in dark leather. He removed the top ledger, which was stenciled A–F on the cover, and crossed the room to his desk. He sat down and opened the ledger to the section flagged with the letter C.

Not quite a year ago, Starbuck had begun organizing his personal rogues' gallery. As a first step, he subscribed to dozens of newspapers throughout the states and territories that constituted the western United States. He next circulated his name throughout the law-enforcement community and got himself on the mailing list for wanted posters; the dodgers on fugitives included across-the-board felonious crime, from horse stealing to murder. Finally, he undertook a program of correspondence with various peace officers and U.S. marshals across the frontier. The response was far more productive than anything he'd imagined. The post office began delivering his mail in a sack.

Quite soon, Verna inherited the project. She read the newspapers, clipping out all articles dealing with criminal activity. She sorted through the wanted posters, cataloguing them by name and locale. And she attended to the correspondence with lawmen, cleverly forging Starbuck's signature whenever he was out of town. The final step, bringing all the intelligence together, involved the four leather-bound ledgers. A page was assigned to each wanted man, and therein were detailed his physical description, his habits and associations, and every known fact regarding his crimes and method of operation. Whenever possible, a tintype or photo was acquired and added to the file. The result was a complete and rather meticulous dossier on nearly three hundred western outlaws. A *Who's Who* of desperate men and desperadoes.

The page on Mike Cassidy was revealing. There was no photo, but listed there were the salient, and somewhat surprising, details. Cassidy was age thirty-eight, with dark hair and brown eyes, and a pronounced scar on his left jawbone. He was five feet ten inches in height, of muscular build, and considered extremely dangerous. A former cowhand, he had turned to rustling in 1879, operating principally in Utah and western Colorado. He was wanted on four counts of cattle rustling, three counts of horse stealing, and one count of murder. The murder victim, a Utah rancher, had been killed attempting to halt a livestock raid. Following the homicide, barely two months past, Cassidy had vanished. His associates were not identified by name, and his only known haunt was the Robbers Roost country of southeastern Utah. There were no further reports on his activities since the murder. He was thought to have skipped Utah, present whereabouts unknown.

Starbuck fished a pack of cigarettes from his coat pocket. He shook one out and struck a match on his thumbnail. After lighting up, he took a deep drag, exhaling little spurts of smoke. He studied the fiery tip of the cigarette a moment, his expression abstracted. Then his eyes went back to the page and stopped. His gaze centered on two words—Robbers Roost.

Several years past, peace officers had discovered the existence of an Outlaw Trail. Extending from northern Arizona to the Canadian border, it traversed the western territories, with three principal hideouts along the route. The first stop, commonly called a station, was Robbers Roost. Bounded by mountains, the desolate wasteland was a maze of canyons and windswept mesas. With only three entrances and a few isolated water holes, the Roost was hazardous country for anyone unfamiliar with its layout. On several occasions, lawmen had penetrated the Roost in pursuit of outlaws. Those who returned told hair-raising stories of being lost and near death before stumbling upon a hidden water hole. Outlaws enjoyed every advantage in the deadly game of hide-and-seek within Robbers Roost.

Farther north, the second station on the trail was Brown's Hole. Located in the northwest corner of Colorado, parts of the Hole extended across the eastern boundary of Utah and the southern boundary of Wyoming. Roughly three hundred miles from Robbers Roost, the Hole was a narrow valley surrounded by mountains. There were only two known entrances into the valley; both of them were down steep and precarious paths from mountain rims to the north and south. Few law officers dared the treacherous passageways, and those who did were confronted by a baffling legal problem. Their quarry eluded capture by skipping back and forth across a patchwork of territorial boundaries. Brown's Hole was a jurisdictional nightmare, where outlaws forever held the edge. Fugitives drifted in and out of the valley almost at will.

The last station on the Outlaw Trail lay some two hundred miles to the northeast. Known simply as Hole-in-the-Wall, it was considered the most formidable of all the hideouts. Located in the barrens of upper Wyoming, the refuge was centered in the foothills of the Big Horn Mountains. According to legend, there was only one entrance, which wound through a narrow gorge into a remote valley. Steeped in mystery, the mountain stronghold was reportedly impregnable. The entrance, by all accounts, could be defended by a mere handful of men. At any given

time, it was believed that upward of a hundred outlaws found sanctuary at Hole-in-the-Wall. Lawmen
never ventured there, and for all practical purposes it
was sacrosanct to the outside world. A true no-man's-
land where death awaited any stranger.

Starbuck took a last drag on his cigarette and
stubbed out the butt in an ashtray. He pulled at his
earlobe, lost in thought. With time and hard-won experience, he had developed the trick of putting himself in the wanted man's boots. All he'd gleaned from
the file—added to that hunter's sixth sense—led to
an obvious conclusion. Mike Cassidy, like most western badmen, was familiar with the hideouts along the
Outlaw Trail. Intelligence reports indicated that rustlers and horse thieves regularly worked the route,
disposing of stolen livestock outside their own homeground. It was reasonable to assume Cassidy had quit
Utah following the murder and journeyed northward
to avoid the hangman's rope. The logical hideout, and
by far the safest, was the last station on the trail. Hole-
in-the-Wall.

One thought led to another, and Starbuck found
himself pondering an unknown. Cassidy was a horse
thief and rustler—no robber—a fact clearly documented in his dossier. Yet he was now charged with
payroll robbery, which seemed somehow out of character. Outlaws generally stuck to one line of work,
and their crimes almost always followed a pattern.
But, of course, the only inviolable rule was that there
were exceptions to the rule. Perhaps, after shifting his
base of operations to Hole-in-the-Wall, Cassidy had
decided on a shift in occupation as well. Even the
lowliest horse thief could aspire to greater things, and
robbery was definitely the more lucrative profession.

All of which would account for the payroll job and dovetail neatly as well with Cassidy's disappearance from Utah. It was, moreover, a matter of proximity. Butte, and the Grubstake Mining Company, were only a few days' ride over the Wyoming line. A quick hit-and-run, within easy striking distance from Hole-in-the-Wall.

Starbuck silently repeated the name to himself. *Hole-in-the-Wall.* There was a foreboding ring to it, and he wondered if all the stories were actually true. In his experience, anything shrouded in mystery and legend generally weighed out to about twelve ounces of bat crap to the pound. The fact that lawmen accepted the stories at face value merely intrigued him all the more. He thought it might be worth the ride just to have a look-see for himself.

Verna appeared in the doorway. She walked to the desk and laid the mining company directory before him. Then she stepped back, hands clasped at her waist.

"You can read it for yourself," she advised him. "But the information you received is essentially correct."

"Tell me about it."

"The Grubstake Mining Company," she recited in a singsong voice, "was organized in August, 1874. The original owners of record were Thomas Benson and Fred Wells. The mine has been in continuous operation, and its principal business is copper. All stock certificates were transferred to Ira Lloyd on July 12, 1879. No current production figures are available."

"About three years," Starbuck mused out loud. "Any indication of the mine's value?"

"None," Verna said briskly. "The company is wholly owned, and no shares are currently listed with the exchange."

"How about Lloyd?" Starbuck persisted. "Anything on him personally?"

"Only his name," Verna remarked. "His mailing address is the same as that of the company."

An instant of weighing and calculation slipped past. Then Starbuck leaned forward and took a sheet of foolscap from the desk drawer. He dipped a pen in the inkwell and hastily scribbled a note. He signed it with a flourish and handed it to Verna.

"Stick that in an envelope and get it over to William Dexter."

"Am I to surmise you've taken the case?"

"Have a gander and see for yourself."

The frown lines around Verna's mouth deepened. She adjusted her pince-nez and held the paper at arm's length. Then she quickly scanned the note.

Assignment accepted. Will depart upon receipt of your check.

Luke Starbuck

"You're really going, then?"

Starbuck smiled. "You might say that."

"Might?" Verna fixed him with a stern look. "I don't understand."

"Neither will the boys at Hole-in-the-Wall."

Chapter Three

Some while later Starbuck left the office. He caught a crosstown trolley and hopped off at Blake Street. Dodging a carriage, he walked to the corner and proceeded along a block of business establishments. He turned into a small shop flanked by a pool hall on one side and a hardware store on the other. The sign on the window was faded and peeling, barely legible.

DANIEL CAMERON
GUNSMITH
PISTOLS—RIFLES—SHOTGUNS

A bell jangled as Starbuck moved through the door. He passed a rack of long guns and walked toward a glass showcase at the rear of the shop. Beyond the showcase was a workbench, and off to one side there was an entrance leading to a back room. A small gray-haired man hurried out, wiping his hands on an oily cloth. He was stooped and wiry, with a face like ancient ivory and a humorous expression suggesting incisive wisdom. His features creased with a wide smile.

"Well, well, who have we here?"

"Afternoon, Daniel."

Starbuck pulled the Colt and thumbed it to half-cock. Though the pistol was in excellent condition, the bluing was worn and the barrel showed signs of wear from years of contact with the holster. He opened the loading gate and slowly spun the cylinder. One at a time, five cartridges spilled out on the counter. With practiced ease, he closed the loading gate and deftly lowered the hammer. Then he laid the pistol before Cameron.

"Time to trade," he said crisply. "I leave tomorrow."

"How were you so sure I'd have the new one finished?"

"Just on a hunch"—Starbuck eyed him keenly—"I'd lay odds you had it ready last week."

Cameron gave him a bewildered look. "Now you're a mind reader!"

"You're an open book, Daniel."

"Am I, now?"

"I've got twenty dollars that says I'm right."

"So tell me, Mr. Detective! What makes you so certain?"

"Simple," Starbuck said confidently. "You won't let go of a gun until someone comes and takes it away from you. You've always got to tinker with it just one day more."

There was no arguing the point. Daniel Cameron was a master gunsmith and a superb craftsman. The inner workings of a firearm were to him like the movement of a fine timepiece. To men who knew weapons, his work bore an invisible, albeit unmistakable, signature. The smoothness of operation and overall functional reliability were hallmarks of his skill. Yet he was a congenital perfectionist; no matter how flawless his work, he was convinced one more day would make it still better. As Starbuck had noted, he surrendered a gun only under duress. The artisan in him simply would not let go.

Cameron laughed, spread his hands. "You know me too well, Luke! Not that it couldn't stand a bit more—"

"Spare me the sermon!" Starbuck interjected. "Trot it on out and let me be the judge."

Cameron muttered something to himself, then turned to the workbench. He opened a drawer and removed a bundle wrapped in dark blue velvet. He crossed back to the counter and placed the bundle on the glass top. Gingerly, like a jeweler displaying a gemstone, he peeled away the velvet folds. His gaze shifted quickly to Starbuck.

The pistol was a Colt's Peacemaker. Chambered for .45 caliber, it had a 4¾-inch barrel with standard sights. The finish was lustrous indigo blue and the grips were gutta-percha, custom-made and deep brown in color.

Apart from its handsome appearance, the gun had been stripped and completely overhauled inside. The sear, as well as the half-cock and full-cock notches on the hammer, had been honed with a fine stone. The result was a trigger pull of slightly more than three pounds, which required only a feathered touch of the trigger finger. The mainspring had also received expert attention, for in a gunfight it was vital that the hammer could be cocked swiftly and with ease. A specially tempered mainspring had been fitted to the gun, thereby enabling the hammer to be eared back with a flick of the thumb. Yet it would still strike the primer with sufficient force to ignite the cartridge.

After a final polishing, all the parts had been rehardened to guarantee strength and prevent excessive wear. The end product was a weapon of incomparable quality. The action was silky smooth, and operation, even under the most adverse conditions, was utterly reliable. The Colt mirrored the artistry of Daniel Cameron.

Starbuck hefted the pistol. His eyes narrowed, and a smile appeared at the corners of his mouth as he tested it for balance. After assuring himself it was unloaded, he thumbed the hammer and touched off the trigger. Then his hand seemed to open and close in rapid succession—working hammer and trigger— and the cylinder made an entire revolution within the span of a few heartbeats. At last, with a look of muted wonder, he turned back to Cameron.

"A helluva job," he said softly. "Your best yet, Daniel."

"Yes, it's special," Cameron said with quiet pride. "I hate to see it go."

"Don't worry." Starbuck chuckled. "I'll put it to good use."

"I never doubted it for a moment, Luke."

Starbuck swiftly loaded the Colt. The cartridges he scooped off the counter were Cameron's handiwork as well. In effect, the slug had been turned upside-down and loaded backward in the casing. The base of the slug, which was blunt and truncated, was now seated in the forward position. Upon impact, the slug would mushroom and expand to roughly half again its normal size. It was an instant manstopper, and a deadly killer.

Holstering the Colt, Starbuck stuck out his hand. "I'm obliged, Daniel."

"Wear it in good health, Luke."

"I'll sure do my damnedest!"

With a wave, Starbuck turned and walked from the shop. Cameron waited until the door closed, then picked up the old Colt. He studied the gun at length, wondering how many men it had sent to the grave. Only Starbuck knew the true number, and he never talked. Which in the end was perhaps the best policy.

A mankiller, Cameron told himself, was entitled to silence.

Starbuck trusted Daniel Cameron as much as he trusted any man. Yet he would never entrust his life to another man's judgment. Nor would he accept on faith alone the workmanship of any gunsmith. Not without performing his own rigorous test.

Across town, he stopped by the hotel and collected a box of cartridges. His next stop was a saloon, where he came away with a bag of empty bottles. From there, he walked to the banks of the Platte River. No one was anywhere in sight and he was reasonably certain of privacy. He emptied the bag on the ground and selected five bottles. One at a time, with a high overhead toss, he pitched them far upstream. The bottles bobbed to the surface and floated toward him.

Starbuck's hand snaked inside his jacket and came out with the Colt. At such times, his mind closed down and his nerves went dead. He willed out all thought and reverted to some trancelike state where he operated on reflex and instinct. Time fragmented into split seconds, and yet there was an icy deliberation suspended within each moment. He simply saw and reacted. There was the gun and the thing he was shooting at and an overwhelming sense of calm. Nothing else.

His arm leveled and the Colt bucked in his hand. The first bottle erupted in a geyser of water and glass. With controlled speed, he swung the Colt in an arc and locked onto the next bottle. His eyes shifted along the barrel—caught within that frozen instant of deliberation—and he feathered the trigger. The second bottle in line exploded. Then the next and the next, and finally the last as the current swept it some yards below his position. From the time he pulled the gun until the moment he lowered his arm, less than five seconds had elapsed. The Colt was quick and smooth, and it shot where he pointed. He was impressed.

Timing himself, Starbuck shucked the empty shells and reloaded. On a measured count of ten, he snapped the loading gate closed and lowered the hammer. His hand moved, and all in a motion he holstered the Colt.

Then he selected five more bottles.

A pale sickle moon lighted the sky. Somewhere in the distance a tower clock struck one as the carriage rolled to a halt before the Brown Palace. The driver jumped down and opened the door. He doffed his hat in an eloquent bow.

Starbuck stepped from the coach. He extended his hand and assisted Lola Montana down. Her eyes were radiant, and in the silty light the mass of golden curls piled atop her head seemed to sparkle with moonbeams. She was attired in a long lavender cape and a full-length gown. For an instant, as she raised her skirts to descend the coach step, a delicate ankle was visible.

She noted his appreciative glance and squeezed his hand. He chuckled lightly, depositing her on the curb. Then he tipped the driver a ten-spot and they turned toward the entrance.

Together, arm in arm, Starbuck and the girl swept into the hotel lobby. The night clerk spotted them and hastily set aside the latest issue of the *Police Gazette*. The sight of Starbuck entering the hotel with a woman on his arm was by now commonplace. Yet the clerk was an ardent admirer of Lola Montana, and he secretly burned with envy that she shared the bed of the hotel's most notorious resident. He quickly moved to a position behind the front desk. No word was spoken, but he met Starbuck's sideways glance with a conspiratorial look. He dipped his head in a slow nod.

Starbuck acknowledged the signal with a faint smile. He crossed the lobby, with Lola clinging to his arm, and entered the elevator. A sleepy bellman waited until they were inside, then closed the gate. The elevator shuddered, responding as the bellman rotated the control lever, and lumbered upward. When they disappeared from view, the night clerk sighed and walked back to his chair. He resumed leafing through the *Police Gazette*, but with dampened interest. He wondered to himself why some men had all the luck.

Upstairs, the elevator rumbled to a halt and the bellman opened the gate. Starbuck bid him goodnight, then led the girl down the hall and unlocked the door to his suite. She preceded him through the foyer and stopped just inside the sitting room. A low table, positioned before the sofa, was laid with fine linen and gleaming silverware. Candles were lighted, and in the center of the table a single yellow rose arched from a stemlike vase. Serving dishes, artfully arranged around the vase, contained a light supper of cold roast squab, brandied pears, and marinated artichoke hearts. A chilled bottle of champagne stood glistening in an ice bucket.

"Ooo Luke!" Lola slipped out of her cape and dropped it on a chair. "All this for me?"

"Nobody else."

Starbuck hung his hat in the foyer and moved into the sitting room. She turned, her expression animated with a sudden verve. Her arms circled his neck and she kissed him soundly on the mouth. Then she pulled back, searching his face with a knowing smile.

"I thought something was up! You and that desk clerk both looked like you had a mouthful of feathers!"

"Don't miss a trick, do you?"

"Not where you're concerned."

"Well, you can thank Joe, the clerk. He's the one who arranged it."

Lola vamped him with a look. "I'd rather thank you."

"You're missing a bet," Starbuck said in a jesting tone. "Joe's sweet on you . . . regular case of puppy love."

"Honey, half the men in Denver are sweet on me!"

Her statement was no idle boast. Lola Montana was the star attraction at the Alcazar Theater, and the toast of Denver's night life. A singer, she was small but nicely put together, with a body like mortal sin. Her jutting breasts tapered to a slim waist and were offset by perfectly rounded hips. Her features were exquisite, with creamy skin and a lush coral mouth that accentuated her high cheekbones. Onstage or off, she was a vision of loveliness, a bawdy nymph bursting with vitality. She was every man's fantasy, and Starbuck's woman.

Yet she was not Starbuck's only woman. She accepted the fact with a certain resignation, and cleverly concealed jealousy. She possessed the wisdom and experience to understand their affair would end if ever she attempted to clip his wings. He slept with other women, but she prudently overlooked those minor lapses; he always returned and she was confident he always would. He was an emotional nomad, wanting no strings and asking none in return. All the same, to the extent he was any woman's man, he was hers. A bond had developed between them, and he let her know in small ways that the attachment was an important part of his life. She cherished the thought.

The champagne and supper were one of those small gestures. Earlier that evening he had appeared at the theater and waited until she finished her midnight performance. Then, without explanation, he'd come backstage and rushed her into changing clothes. At the time, he had been very mysterious, and evaded her questions with a charm normally hidden beneath layers of reserve. Now, suddenly, she understood. The candlelight and rose, all the little added touches, were by way of an affectionate goodbye. He would be gone when she awoke in the morning.

"You sly devil!" Her voice was light and mocking. "You're taking off on a case—aren't you?"

"Damn!" Starbuck watched her with an indulgent smile. "I thought I had you fooled."

"Fat chance!" Lola gave him a bright, theatrical

smile. "Would it do me any good to ask where you're headed?"

"I never fib to ladies"—Starbuck smiled gently—"unless I've got no choice."

Lola wrinkled her nose. "Any idea how long you'll be gone?"

"No longer than it takes."

"Well, don't take too long, lover. I'm liable to start drinking alone, or biting my nails."

"No cause for worry," Starbuck said lightly. "I generally get it done one way or the other."

All of which was true. Lola was concerned but not overly alarmed by the nature of his work. She knew every inch of his body, and she'd personally satisfied herself that it was unmarred by bullet or knife wounds. Added to the number of men he'd killed, it revealed much about his ability to survive. She believed him immune to harm.

"Let's forget I asked." Her lips curved in a teasing smile. "I'll know you're back when I see you. How's that?"

"Sounds fair." Starbuck met her gaze, found something merry lurking there. "How about some champagne? I had this spread laid out special."

"Not now." A vixen look touched her eyes. "Later."

She stretched voluptuously and held out her arms. Her low-cut gown dipped lower, exposing the swell of her breasts. Her laughter was musical and her expression suddenly gleamed with mischief.

"I want my dessert first."

Starbuck marveled again at her almost total lack of inhibition. Her passion was wild and atavistic, and her a sexual appetite was easily a match for his own.

He lifted her in his arms and carried her toward the bedroom. She playfully nibbled his earlobe, laughed a low throaty laugh.

A spill of light from the door flooded the darkened room. He lowered her onto the bed and within a few moments they were naked. She snuggled close in his embrace, her lips moist and inviting. Her hands cupped his face, caressing the hard line of his jaw, and a strange thing happened. She trembled, staring intently into his eyes, and almost spoke. Then she shuddered and her fingernails pierced his back like talons. She pulled him to her.

Their tongues met and dueled. His hand covered one of her breasts, and the nipple swelled instantly. Then his fingers drifted downward, probed the curly delta where her thighs forked. She was damp and yielding, and she uttered a low moan, thrusting against him. Her hand went to his manhood, grasped that hard questing part of him, and stroked it eagerly. For several moments they kissed and fondled, until finally, aroused and aching, she could wait no longer. Her mouth opened in a gasping cry of urgency.

"Ohhh Luke! Now! *Now!*"

Chapter Four

Starbuck left the hotel shortly before sunrise. He took the backstairs and made his way unseen to the basement furnace room. There he exited through a rear door into the alley.

The purpose of his secrecy was twofold. By leaving the hotel unobserved, his departure from Denver would go unnoticed. Only after he'd been gone a few days would he be missed. There was, additionally, an even more critical factor. He was traveling in disguise.

Overall, his appearance was that of an easterner. He was attired in a sedate, expensively tailored tweed suit, topped off by a fashionable beige fedora. He wore spectacles, with heavy wire frames and lenses of plain glass. His shoes were kid leather, polished to a high gloss, and specially constructed. The instep of the left shoe had been built up slightly more than an inch, which had the immediate effect of shortening his left leg. The result was a pronounced limp and a somewhat halting gait. All in all, he looked like a bookish intellectual with a mild deformity.

The publicity surrounding many of his past cases had robbed Starbuck of anonymity. His photo, which had appeared in newspapers throughout the West, made his face known wherever he traveled. Working undercover, it thereby became imperative that he operate in disguise. Early on, when he'd begun his career as a range detective, he had discovered a certain gift for subterfuge and guile. He possessed a streak of the actor, and over the years he had played a wide variety of roles. By turn, he'd posed as a whoremonger and grifter, Bible salesman and drummer, and an assortment of outlaws ranging from horse thief to bank robber. Every assignment offered a unique challenge, and his natural flair for disguise enabled him to create a character suitable to the occasion. He was, in a very real sense, a one-man stock company.

Not unlike a sleight-of-hand artist, Starbuck used misdirection to great effect. The externals—outward appearance and physical quirks—created an illusion. What people saw was the superficial, the obvious; their eye was misdirected from the reality underneath. The deception was then rounded out with mannerisms and speech patterns peculiar to the character he portrayed. A general rule was the simpler the better, with just a touch of the bizarre. Added to the disguise, a credible cover story provided the final twist. His survival rested on the skill of his performance, and once he'd assumed a role, Luke Starbuck simply ceased to exist. He submerged himself, mentally and physically, within the character of the moment.

To enhance security, Starbuck followed still another cardinal rule. He never divulged professional secrets to anyone, whether client or friend. His disguise, the cover story, even the alias he employed, was a matter of strictest confidence. Verna Phelps, whose loyalty was unquestionable, knew only the broad outlines of his assignment. Lola Montana and Daniel Cameron, while trustworthy, were told nothing. What they didn't know couldn't be repeated; the most innocent remark, whether about the case itself or his destination, would find a ready audience in Denver's Tenderloin. From there, the word would spread by moccasin telegraph to every corner of the underworld. The upshot would jeopardize not only the assignment, but perhaps his life as well. He operated on the principle that a secret, once shared, was no longer a secret.

Nor was he any less closemouthed with clients. He operated on his own terms, take it or leave it. Once he'd accepted a case, there was seldom any further communication. He submitted no reports, and revealed nothing with regard to his methods or his strategy. To the extent possible, he kept the client in the dark until the assignment was concluded. He was paid to get results, and when the final tally was taken, the results spoke for themselves. How he went about it was his own business.

The assignment undertaken today was no different. Beyond Starbuck's terse note, there had been no further communication with William Dexter. The lawyer had doubtless notified Ira Lloyd, the mine owner in Butte, as to the disposition of the case. That seemed reasonable to assume since Dexter's check for five thousand dollars had arrived at the office late yesterday afternoon. Yet, from this point onward, the lawyer would know nothing. He might surmise Starbuck had departed for Wyoming, and in that he would be correct. Anything else would remain privileged information.

The morning train for Cheyenne was scheduled to depart at six o'clock. A cautious man, Starbuck allowed himself an hour's leeway. Upon emerging from the alleyway, he crossed the street and walked west from the hotel. He spent the next thirty minutes circling and doubling back, constantly looking over his shoulder. There was no reason to believe he was being followed; but the practice was by now a deeply ingrained habit. He never took anything for granted, and unless unavoidable, he never left anything to chance. Today was no exception.

By sunup, he felt confident he wasn't being tailed. He reversed course as an orange ball of fire crested the horizon. The city was slowly coming to life, and street traffic increased markedly as he hurried toward Union Station. Less than three minutes before train time, he moved through the depot and walked directly to the passenger platform. The locomotive was chuffing steam, and late arrivals were rushing to scramble aboard. He'd cut it close, but he knew there would be no problem purchasing a ticket from the conductor. Stepping onto the last coach, he stowed his valise in an overhead rack and took a window seat. The train got under way within a matter of moments.

Starbuck had the seat to himself, and he sat for a while watching the mountains. Always a spectacular sight at sunrise, the Rockies seemed to mirror every color in the spectrum. There was a stately grandeur to the scene that never failed to impress him. Still, as the train chugged northward out of Denver, his thoughts slowly turned to the task ahead. He pulled the fedora down over his eyes and pretended to snooze. Yet his mind was very much on Cheyenne. And the Wyoming Stock Growers Association.

The plan formulated by Starbuck was necessarily sketchy. Mike Cassidy, the outlaw he'd been hired to track down, was almost a cipher. With no photo, and no positive means of identification, the assignment definitely posed a challenge. The problem was compounded by still another unknown, Hole-in-the-Wall. All of which meant Starbuck was operating largely in the blind. Yet he was by no means at a loss for a place to start. His investigation would begin with Nathaniel Boswell.

A mankiller of some repute, Nat Boswell was widely respected throughout Wyoming. His service as a peace officer began in 1868, when the Union Pacific was laying track west and Cheyenne was a lawless hellhole. Boswell aroused the citizenry and organized a vigilante committee, which was responsible for ridding the town of outlaws and troublemakers. Shortly thereafter, the territorial governor appointed him sheriff of Albany County. With the commission, he became the chief lawman of a vast region stretching from Colorado to Montana. After several terms in office, he went on to become a detective and undercover operative for the Union Pacific. Only recently, he had been appointed director of the Wyoming Stock Growers Association. Under his command was a force of five range detectives, and he was charged with routing bands of rustlers who preyed on association herds. He was, according to all reports, eminently good at the job. The number of cow thieves killed or hanged had risen dramatically in the last few months. His detectives were not noted for bringing wanted men in alive.

Over the past year, Starbuck had carried on extensive correspondence with Boswell. In organizing his rogues' gallery, he had contacted the Wyoming lawman and requested assistance. Boswell readily cooperated, and in the intervening months, he had become an invaluable source of hard intelligence. The information he forwarded to Denver was concise and timely, and indicated a deep insight into the mentality of outlaws. Though they had never met, Starbuck considered him a top-notch detective. He was, moreover, a legend on the High Plains. No one purposely crossed paths with Nat Boswell.

Starbuck's plan was simple, though somewhat devious. Without revealing his identity, or the nature of his assignment, he intended to pump the stock detective dry of information. His cover story was a corker, and he thought it would play well in Cheyenne. All the more important, he believed it would appeal to Nat Boswell's sense of personal esteem.

And thereby open the door to Hole-in-the-Wall.

Cheyenne was a bustling plains metropolis. The capital of Wyoming Territory, with a population of nearly twenty thousand, it was a major railhead and center of commerce. As a stopover for those en route to the Dakota gold camps, it was also a beehive of trade. On the southside, bordering the railroad tracks, gambling dens and dance halls, variety theaters and bawdy-houses comprised a thriving vice district. Farther uptown, the business district was packed with stores and hotels, restaurants and saloons, several banks, and the territory's leading newspaper. For good reason, Cheyenne had been dubbed the Magic City of the Plains.

Starbuck went directly from the depot to one of the uptown hotels. There he engaged a room for the night and left his valise with the bellman. Then he inquired the location of the Wyoming Stock Growers Association. The desk clerk obligingly pointed him in the right direction. On the street again, he walked toward the town's main intersection.

Some minutes later he went past a bank and rounded the corner. An outside staircase led to an office on the second floor. Upstairs, he entered and found himself in a room with the plain look of a monk's cell. There was a single desk, a couple of file cabinets, and several wooden armchairs. On one wall was a large map of Wyoming Territory. Seated behind the desk was a man who seemed fitted to the sparse accommodations.

Somewhere in his early forties, Nat Boswell was lynx-eyed and whipcord lean. He had gnarled hands, a straight, razored mouth, and features the color of ancient saddle leather. He assessed Starbuck in a single glance. The eastern clothes were duly noted, and his gaze lingered a moment on the gimpy leg. Then, without expression, he looked up and waited.

"Hello there!" Starbuck fixed his face in a jaunty smile and limped across the room. "By any chance, would you be Mr. Nathaniel K. Boswell?"

"Who's asking?"

"Edward Farnum." Starbuck beamed. "I'm with the *Police Gazette*."

"A reporter?"

"Chief correspondent and associate editor."

Boswell seemed to thaw a little. "What can I do for you?"

"You're Mr. Boswell!" Starbuck grabbed his hand and pumped vigorously. "It's an honor and a pleasure, Mr. Boswell. I simply can't tell you how delighted I am!"

"That a fact?" Boswell waved him to a chair. "What brings you to Cheyenne?"

"Why, you do, Mr. Boswell I'm writing a series of articles on western lawmen, and the paper sent me here expressly to interview you."

"Do tell." Boswell sounded flattered. "What sort of series?"

"The crème de la crème!" Starbuck struck a dramatic pose. "Bill Tilghman of Dodge City. Heck Thomas in Indian Territory. John Armstrong of the Texas Rangers. And Nat Boswell—the Wyoming Avenger!"

"Wyoming Avenger, huh?" Boswell grinned, clearly pleased with the ring of it. "You've got me traveling in pretty fancy company."

"Not at all!" Starbuck observed grandly. "You are too modest by far, Mr. Boswell. In the East your name is legend—without peer!"

"Well—" Boswell tried for humility. "I'm just doing my job, that's all."

"Indeed you are! And that is precisely the angle I wish to explore in the article. A man of noble purpose battling the western Visigoths!"

"Who?"

"Marauders!" Starbuck explained. "Cattle rustlers and horse thieves and gunmen. The outlaw element!"

Boswell nodded wisely. "Wyoming's got its share, no two ways about it."

"Well, now!" Starbuck pulled out a pad and pencil. "Perhaps we could get down to cases. Would you say, Mr. Boswell, that cattle rustlers are Wyoming's principal problem at the moment?"

"I would," Boswell affirmed. "That's why the big ranchers got together and formed the Stock Growers Association."

"A classic citizens' action"—Starbuck scribbled furiously—"when organized law enforcement fails to mete out justice. And might I assume your results to date are encouraging?"

"I reckon you could say that."

"Perhaps some figures," Starbuck said with an expansive gesture. "How many have you hanged or killed in gun battles? Our readers do love the blood and gore of western expediency."

Boswell eyed him warily. "I'd like to accommodate you, Mr. Farnum. But there's certain things the association don't want bandied about. Might give folks the wrong idea."

"A pity." Starbuck feigned disappointment. "However, in general, it would be fair to say you have depleted their ranks. Is that correct?"

"Mostly." Boswell wrestled with himself a moment, then shrugged. "Course, you no sooner weed out one bunch and another crop springs up. It's a job that never gets done."

Starbuck paused, thoughtfully tapped the pencil on his notepad. "Perhaps we could draw an illustration between today and how it was when you were appointed director. In your own words, how would you characterize the situation, Mr. Boswell?"

"Under control," Boswell said firmly. "We've got 'em on the run and that's the way we aim to keep it. Where there's cows, there'll always be rustling, and nobody's gonna stop it cold. But we do a damnsight better job than most."

"Bully!" Starbuck chortled, writing it all down. "I can see it now! A bold headline! Boswell Routs Wyoming Rustlers! Capital stuff, Mr. Boswell. Really first-rate!"

"Hmmm." Boswell studied him with mock gravity. "Well, don't go overboard, Mr. Farnum. Like I said, we've still got our work cut out for us."

"Now that you mention it," Starbuck inquired innocently, "we've heard some rather strange reports about a place—I believe I have the name correct—Hole-in-the-Wall?"

Boswell studied him with some surprise. "What about it?"

"I'm asking you!" Starbuck appeared bemused. His gaze was inquisitive, oddly perplexed. "Are the rumors true? Is it a haven for outlaws and desperadoes?"

"Yes and no." Boswell regarded him dourly. "We get 'em when they come out of Hole-in-the-Wall. Once they're in there, we bide our time and play a waiting game."

"Are you saying"—Starbuck peered over his glasses with owlish scrutiny—"you never follow them into Hole-in-the-Wall?"

"Yeah." Boswell's frown deepened. "That's about the size of it."

Starbuck looked thoroughly mystified. "May I ask why not?"

" 'Cause there's only one way in and one way out. And there's men guarding the entrance night and day. It'd take an army to get through, and even then they'd be cut to ribbons."

"So the reports are correct?" Starbuck asked. "It's a stronghold, some sort of mountain fortress?"

"Close enough," Boswell grated. "What you've got is a valley surrounded by mountains. The mountains are impassable and there's only a narrow canyon leading into the valley. Call it whatever you will, it's a tough nut to crack."

"How perfectly astounding!" Starbuck marveled. "You've seen it for yourself, then?"

Boswell blinked, sat erect. "No, not just exactly."

"I don't mean the valley," Starbuck added hastily. "I was referring to the canyon . . . the Hole-in-the-Wall itself."

"Answer's still the same," Boswell said flatly. "I never looked it over personal."

"Never?" Starbuck repeated incredulously. "Why on earth not?"

Boswell pulled in his neck and stared across the desk with a bulldog scowl. "Mister, I don't care much for your tone. You're just a mite too goddamn pushy for my taste."

"Pleeeze!" Starbuck fluttered weakly. "I wasn't questioning your courage, Mr. Boswell. Good Lord, no! I was merely asking why you've never gone there . . . just taken a peek?"

"Suicide's not my game."

"I beg your pardon?"

"Tell you a little story." Boswell's voice dropped. "Back in the summer of '78 a couple of Union Pacific detectives trailed some robbers into Hole-in-the-Wall. They never been heard from since. The same thing happened to a deputy sheriff who was long on grit and short on brains. You get my drift?"

"Indeed I do!" Starbuck looked properly impressed. "You're saying those who tried sacrificed their lives in the effort. So, as a result, peace officers very prudently avoid it altogether."

"I think you got the picture, Mr. Farnum."

"Out of curiosity"—Starbuck glanced at the large wall map—"exactly where is Hole-in-the-Wall?"

Boswell rose and moved around his desk to the

map. He traced a route north to Fort Laramie, then indicated a stretch along the Oregon Trail, and finally stopped at the foothills of the Big Horn Mountains. He rapped a spot on the map.

"That'll give you a rough idea."

"Good heavens," Starbuck breathed softly. "It really is godforsaken, isn't it?"

"Smack-dab in the middle of nowhere, and that's a fact."

"What about ranchers?" Starbuck scanned the map. "Or homesteaders? Has anyone dared settle up there?"

"Oh, there's some," Boswell allowed. "The closest one to Hole-in-the-Wall is a fellow named Ed Houk. He's got a fair-sized spread on Buffalo Creek. That's just south of the canyon I told you about."

Starbuck made a mental note of the name. Then, playing to Boswell's touchy pride, he went on with the interview. He jotted down every word in copious detail, acting the part of a journalist hot on the trail of a story. At last, with much handshaking and profuse thanks, he took his leave. On the way out the door, he had to suppress a smile. His hunch had proved dead on the money. Lawmen, solely for their own devices, had joined fact and fable in an unholy alliance.

Nobody knew beans about Hole-in-the-Wall.

Chapter Five

Early next morning Starbuck emerged from the hotel. He was still attired in the tweed suit and fedora, and he stood for a monet surveying the street. Then he turned and walked toward the train depot.

Cheyenne was a sprawling hodgepodge of buildings. Hammered together on the windswept plains, it was a curious admixture of cowtown and citified elegance. The Union Pacific had transformed it into a hub of trade and commerce, with an ever expanding business district. As the territorial capital, the city had slowly assumed an aura of respectability and cultivation. Yet it was also the major railhead for Wyoming's vast cattle industry.

Every summer herds were trailed into Cheyenne from ranches all across the High Plains. After being sold to cattle brokers, the cows were shipped east for slaughter. A great deal of money exchanged hands, and in the process, the town prospered. However progressive, the political bigwigs and local merchants catered to cattlemen for the best of reasons. Cows were big business, the mainstay of Cheyenne's economic growth.

Centered around the train depot were various enterprises related to the cattle trade. The vice district, where a carnival atmosphere prevailed during trailing

season, was devoted exclusively to the rough tastes
of cowhands. Nearby were holding pens and loading
yards, along with several livestock dealers. Horses,
usually trailed overland from Texas, were yet another
flourishing business in Cheyenne. Wyoming cattlemen found it easier to buy than breed, and thereby
created a market. Good saddle mounts were in constant demand.

Starbuck chose one of the larger livestock dealers. He entered the office, and was greeted by a
paunchy, whey-faced man with muttonchop whiskers.
The dealer gave his eastern clothes a slow once-over,
but asked no questions. A sale was a sale, and he
expressed no curiosity as to why a greenhorn wanted
a saddle horse. He led the way to a large stock pen
outside.

Something more than a hundred horses stood
munching hay scattered on the ground. Starbuck circled the fence, checking conformation and general
condition. After several minutes, he selected a blood
bay, with black mane and tail. A gelding, the animal
was barrel-chested, standing fifteen hands high and
weighing well over a thousand pounds. His hide glistened in the sun like dark blood on polished redwood,
and he looked built for stamina.

A stablehand roped the bay and led him from the
pen. Starbuck inspected his hooves and teeth, then
asked to have him saddled. Stepping aboard, he rode
the horse to the edge of town and brougt him back at
a full gallop. The bay was spirited, though not high-
strung, and exhibited an even disposition. He possessed speed and catlike agility, and plenty of bottom
for endurance over a long haul. Starbuck decided to
look no further.

"Nice pick." The dealer nodded sagely. "You got an eye for horseflesh."

"Thank you." Starbuck took out a handkerchief and began wiping dust from his glasses. "What price are you asking?"

The dealer quoted a figure nearly double the going rate. Starbuck acted gullible, but dickered awhile merely for effect. At last, when the dealer offered to throw in a saddle, he allowed himself to be cheated by some fifty dollars. He paid in cash, and rented a stall in the dealer's livery stable. With a bill of sale in his pocket, he headed back uptown. The dealer looked pleased as punch.

Starbuck's next stop was a store frequented by cowhands. He'd already worked out a disguise and a plausible cover story for Hole-in-the-Wall. Now he needed a wardrobe to fit the part. Since outlaws traveled light, he planned nothing elaborate in the way of camp gear. His purpose was to create yet another illusion—a man on the run.

The store was on the order of a general emporium. Apart from clothing, the stock included saddles and tinned goods and a wide assortment of firearms. The interior smelled of leather and gun oil and musty woolens. A clerk bustled forward, eyeballing Starbuck's eastern getup with a quizzical look. He gave the impression he was biting his tongue. Yet, like the livestock dealer, he asked no questions.

With some care, Starbuck selected an outfit. He stuck to serviceable range duds, nothing fancy. To a linsey shirt and whipcord trousers, he added a mackinaw, plain high-topped boots, and a dun-colored Stetson. Then he picked out a blanket and bedroll tarp, along with the bare essentials in camp gear. A supply of tobacco and some victuals completed his shopping list.

The clothing was new and looked fresh off the shelves. Still, he saw that as no insurmountable problem. By necessity, he'd long ago perfected the knack of aging clothing so that it had a worn appearance. Then, too, he would be several days on the trail, and sleeping on the ground. By the time he arrived at Hole-in-the-Wall, the problem would have resolved itself. His clothes would look as rank as he smelled.

On impulse, he bought a belt studded with silver conchas and a leather vest. The combination added a showy touch, suitable to the character he had in mind. Then, turning toward the counter, his eye fell on a rack of long guns. He abruptly recalled one last item.

"I'll need a rifle," he said, motioning to the clerk. "Let me see something with a little range to it . . . no carbines."

"Oh, you're a hunter!" the clerk said brightly. "I wondered what you were outfitting yourself for."

"You guessed it." Starbuck smiled. "Thought I'd try my hand at some big game."

"Well, now, I might have something that'll interest you! Yessir, I surely might!"

"Winchester?"

"No, sir." The clerk pulled a rifle from the rack and held it out. "A Colt Lightning! It's new, not even in production yet. The factory released a few prototype models—just to test the market."

"I thought Colt was strictly pistols."

"Apparently they're after some of Winchester's business. Here, try it on for size! I guarantee you, it's a humdinger!"

Starbuck hefted the rifle. The balance and workmanship were superb. A pump-action repeater, the stock and foregrip were dark-grained walnut, and the octagon barrel was twenty-six inches long. A tubular cartridge magazine extended beneath the barrel; a backward stroke of the foregrip ejected the spent shell and a forward stroke chambered a fresh round. The sights were quick to the eye, with a buckhorn rear sight and a gold-beaded front sight.

Stepping away from the counter, Starbuck tested the sights and found the pickup amazingly swift. He jacked the slide-action several times, and discovered operation was a shade faster than a lever-action. He swung the rifle in an arc—sighting on a tin of peaches—and squeezed the trigger. The let-off was crisp and light to the touch. He smiled, and turned back to the clerk.

"Got a nice feel."

"My sentiments exactly." The clerk lowered his voice. "Most of our customers were weaned on lever-actions, and won't even take a second look. I can see you're a man who's not stuck in a rut."

Starbuck inspected the rifle closer. "What caliber?"

".50-95!" The clerk grinned as though sharing a secret. "It packs a real wallop!"

"I'd say so," Starbuck observed quietly. "How many rounds does it hold?"

"Ten."

The clerk took a box of cartridges off the shelf. He opened it and held up a shell. The massive fifty-caliber slug was seated in a brass casing almost as long as his finger. He slowly shook his head.

"I'd hate to get hit with that."

"You and me both," Starbuck agreed. "How is it on accuracy?"

"According to the factory, it's a sizzler clean out to five hundred yards."

"I suppose that's far enough."

"Yessir, it's a rare shot at that range!"

Starbuck laid the rifle on the counter. "I'll take it."

"I believe you've made a wise choice, Mr.—?"

"Farnum," Starbuck replied. "How are you fixed for cartridges?"

"We have three boxes in stock."

"I'll take those, too. And a saddle boot for the rifle."

"Very well, Mr. Farnum," the clerk said pleasantly. "Now, could I interest you in a pistol? We have an excellent selection."

"With that rifle"—Starbuck mugged, hands outstretched—"who needs a pistol?"

"Who indeed, Mr. Farnum? Yessir, who indeed!"

Starbuck again paid in cash. Then he asked the clerk to package everything and have it delivered to the hotel. On his way out the door he checked his watch and saw it was approaching the noon hour. Outside, he turned upstreet and went looking for a café.

To Starbuck, food in itself was unimportant. He appreciated—and distinguished between—good cooking and poor cooking. He much preferred tender beefsteak, properly juicy and rare, to a piece of meat charred rawhide tough. Yet, in the overall scheme of things, the culinary fixings were of no great consequence. For him, eating was simply a bodily function, much like a bowel movement. He ate because his body demanded sustenance, and no elaborate ritual was attached to the eating. A minute after shoving his plate away, the meal was forgotten. Good, bad, or indifferent . . . food was food.

Halfway up the block Starbuck spotted a greasy spoon. Walking toward it, he suddenly pulled up short when the bat-wing doors of a saloon burst open. A cowhand lurched outside and stepped directly into his path. The man was tall and burly, dressed in faded range clothes, and to all appearances stumbling drunk. His features were set in a quarrelsome scowl.

Before Starbuck could step aside, the cowhand bulled into him. The force of the collision knocked him upside the wall of the saloon. With a violent oath, the cowhand turned on him.

"Who you shovin'?"

"Sorry." Starbuck wanted no trouble, and tried to ease past. "No harm intended."

"The hell you say! Think you own the gawddamn sidewalk?"

"Look, friend—"

"Friend!" the cowhand bellowed. "Who you callin' friend, you pansy sonovabitch!"

"I only—"

The cowhand launched a looping roundhouse. Starbuck's countermove was one of sheer reflex. He slipped inside the haymaker and exploded a left hook to the jaw. The punch rocked the cowhand and he reeled backward off the boardwalk. A streetside hitch rack saved him from falling, and he seemed to shake off the effects of the blow. Then, too quick for the eye, a gun appeared from inside his jacket. He snapped off a lightning shot.

Starbuck got lucky. He was a beat behind, but the

cowhand hurried the shot. The slug tore through the sleeve of Starbuck's coat and thunked into the wall. He pulled the Colt, thumbing the hammer in the same motion, and fired. A bright red dot blossomed on the cowhand's shirtfront. The impact of the blunt-nosed slug slammed him into the hitch rack. He hung there a moment, then his legs buckled and his sphincter voided in death. He slumped to the ground without a sound.

A wisp of smoke curled from the barrel of Starbuck's pistol. He was aware of voices and people crowding the street. Yet his gaze was on the dead man, and in some dim corner of his mind a question slowly took shape. The man was uncommonly sudden with a gun, too sudden.

He wondered how a ragtail cowhand got so fast.

"You say you never saw him before?"

"Never."

"So he jumped you out of the clear blue?"

"It would appear that way."

Amos Rodman, town marshal of Cheyenne, sat across the desk from Starbuck. Summoned to the scene of the shooting, he had questioned several eyewitnesses and ordered the body removed to a funeral parlor. Then he'd taken Starbuck into custody and marched him back to the city jail. Now, with a cigar wedged in the corner of his mouth, he tilted back in his chair. His expression was one of puzzlement.

"Why would he do that—jump a stranger?"

Starbuck warned himself to go slow. The interrogation was something more than mere formality. He was still posing as an easterner, and that fact clearly troubled the marshal. He lifted his hands in a shrug.

"The man was drunk and belligerent. I can only surmise he was spoiling for a fight."

"Funny thing," Rodman said lazily. "The barkeep in that saloon said he never even had a drink. Walked in off the street, and a couple of minutes later he walks right out again. How do you explain that?"

"I wouldn't try." Starbuck gave him a weak smile. "Who knows what prompts men to violence?"

"Good question," Rodman remarked. "Suppose you tell me. If it wasn't liquor . . . what was it?"

"I'm afraid I have no answer to that, Marshal."

Rodman lowered his chair and leaned forward. He took Starbuck's Colt off the desktop and slowly examined it. His brow wrinkled in a frown.

"That's a mighty fancy gun for a pilgrim."

Starbuck played dumb. "Pilgrim?"

"You told me you're a reporter."

"That's correct."

"An *eastern* reporter!"

"I fail to see the connection."

"Do you?" Rodman scoffed. "You've got a hair-trigger pistol and a slicker'n-grease crossdraw holster. Wouldn't you say that's a pretty peculiar rig for a reporter?"

"Not necessarily." Starbuck hesitated, chose his words with care. "A man versed in weapons should carry the best."

"You're versed, all right!" Rodman growled. "Too damn versed! Unless maybe you're not what you claim."

Starbuck looked bewildered. "I beg your pardon?"

"Maybe you're a gambler or a bunco artist. You could've gigged that fellow in some other trail town and he just accidentally happened across you today. It's got all the earmarks of somebody settlin' a personal score."

"That's ridiculous!"

"Folks don't generally go around pullin' guns on a stranger."

"Well, I assure you he was a stranger to me."

"Yeah?" Rodman inquired skeptically. "Then how come he tied into you so fast?"

"I have no idea," Starbuck said lamely. "After all, he picked the fight . . . not me."

"You ended it, though! That's what we're talkin' about here."

"I merely defended myself, Marshal."

"So you keep sayin'."

"Good Lord!" Starbuck said indignantly. "Any number of people substantiated my story! You have eyewitness accounts of everything that transpired. What more do you want?"

"For one thing," Rodman countered, "I want to know considerable more about you."

"Then I suggest you check with Nathaniel Boswell. I came here to interview him, and he found my credentials perfectly satisfactory. I'm quite confident Mr. Boswell will vouch for me."

"Oh, I'll check around." Rodman paused, gave him a dull stare. "Meantime, I wouldn't want you to plan on leavin' town."

"May I ask why?"

"Suppose we just say something smells fishy."

"How long will I be detained?"

"All depends," Rodman said evasively. "I'll let you know."

"Very well." Starbuck rose, stood fidgeting with

a hangdog look. "Since I'm not under arrest, I would appreciate the return of my gun."

"Help yourself," Rodman said, motioning toward the pistol. "Course, I ought to warn you. We've got a city ordinance against carryin' concealed weapons."

"Someone should have informed the dead man."

"I'm informing you and that's enough!"

"And in the event he has some friends who also ignore your ordinance? What would you suggest then, Marshal?"

"I'd suggest you stick to your hotel room."

"How comforting."

Starbuck holstered the Colt and walked to the door. With his hand on the knob, he turned and looked back over his shoulder. "One last question."

"Shoot."

"The deceased—" Starbuck made an empty gesture. "Were you able to identify him?"

"Nope," Rodman said without inflection. "There were no papers on the body, and no one recalled seein' him before today."

"Perhaps he worked for one of the cattle outfits."

"Possible," Rodman conceded. "Or he could've been a drifter."

"In which case, we'll never know."

"I wouldn't bet it either way, Mr. Farnum."

The comment gave Starbuck all the clue he needed. Outside, walking toward the hotel, he told himself the bet was a lead-pipe cinch. Marshal Amos Rodman would have a wire off to the *Police Gazette* within the hour. Then he would start nosing around town, asking questions. By tomorrow, maybe sooner, he would discover that an easterner wearing glasses had bought a horse, along with outdoors gear and a rifle. All that, added to a reply from the *Police Gazette*, would lead to more questions. Questions Starbuck couldn't afford to have asked, or answered. Which meant nightfall was the deadline.

By then, he had to be long gone from Cheyenne.

Chapter Six

Starbuck rode north toward Fort Laramie. He used the stars for a compass and he rode straight through the night. He left behind nothing of Edward Farnum.

Earlier, in his hotel room, Starbuck had laid the reporter to rest. The glasses and eastern clothing, along with the specially built shoes, were stowed in his valise. His new disguise was less elaborate, but no less effective. From the valise, he took a master-work of dental handicraft. On the order of a false tooth, it was actually an enameled sleeve, colored a dark nut brown. Custom-fitted, it slipped over his left front tooth and was secured much like a partial bridge. To all appearances a dead tooth, it was yet another exercise in misdirection, and an immediate eye-stopper. People saw the blackened tooth and were distracted from the man.

The balance of his disguise relied on clothing and whiskery stubble. His beard, which grew rapidly, would alter the set of his features. By the time he arrived at Hole-in-the-Wall, he would have sprouted a mustache and a full growth along his chin and jaw-line. The conchas belt, added to the range clothes and vest, would complete the transformation. A dead tooth, nestled in a coppery beard, would erase any vestige of Luke Starbuck. What emerged would be a whiskery, rough-garbed hardcase. An outlaw who called himself Arapahoe Smith.

Starbuck's departure from Cheyenne had gone smoothly. Shortly after dark, he left money on the washstand for his hotel bill. Then he knotted bed-sheets into a rope and went out the window of his second-floor room. The valise, which contained the remnants of Edward Farnum, was dumped in an alley trash heap. Sticking to back streets, he then made his way to the livery stable. The blood bay gelding was saddled without awakening the night hostler. All his gear was crammed into saddlebags; then the rifle scabbard and bedroll were lashed down securely. Once outside, he mounted and circled west of town. There, he fixed on the North Star and booted the horse into a steady lope. No trace of him or the direction he rode remained behind. He vanished, unseen, into the night.

By sundown of the second day Starbuck sighted Fort Laramie. The army post was situated at the junc-ture of the Laramie and North Platte rivers. Originally built by fur traders, it was taken over by the military when emigrant trains began the westward migration. Thereafter it served as a shakedown point for those traveling the Oregon Trail. The Bozeman Trail, mapped out when gold was discovered in Montana, also passed through Fort Laramie. Stretching north and west, a chain of forts was then constructed to combat the Sioux and other hostile tribes. Yet, for all their number, these forts were merely outposts in the wilderness. Fort Laramie remained the crossroads of the western plains.

Avoiding the fort, Starbuck rode on a few miles and pitched camp. The next morning he struck out along the Oregon Trail, which followed the North Platte in a westerly direction. He would have made better time overland, for the trail twisted and turned in concert with the winding river. But he was on unfamiliar ground, and dared not overshoot a vital landmark, known generally as the Upper Crossing. There, on a dogleg in the river, the Oregon Trail intersected the old Bridger Trail. Little traveled, the trail had been blazed many years before by the mountain man and scout Jim Bridger. Angling northwest from the river, it meandered through the Big Horn Basin and ultimately linked up with the Bozeman Trail. Along the way, it also skirted the only known entrance to Hole-in-the-Wall.

Three days out of Fort Laramie, Starbuck turned onto the Bridger Trail. Ahead lay the foothills of the Big Horn Range and an ocean of grassland. The basin, with distant mountains on either side, stretched endlessly to the horizon. The landscape evoked a sense of something lost forever. Nothing moved as far as the eye could see, and hardly a bush or a tree was visible in the vast emptiness sweeping northward. Earth and sky were mixed with deafening silence, almost as though, in some ancient age, the plains had frozen motionless for all time. A gentle breeze, like the wispy breath of a ghost, rippled over the tall grass, disturbing nothing. It was a land of sun and solitude, a lonesome land. A land where man somehow seemed the intruder.

Only a few years ago it had been the land of the Sioux. From the North Platte in Wyoming to the Rosebud in Montana, a swath of grassland over a hundred miles long teemed with buffalo. The vast seas of bluestem and needlegrass were the natural rangeland of a herd numbering in the millions. Then, in quick succession, gold and the lure of free land brought a flood tide of emigrants. Not far behind were the hide hunters, openly encouraged by the army, whose leaders sanctioned the slaughter. Within a decade, the great buffalo herds—the Indians' commissary—were no more. Nor were the Sioux themselves any longer in evidence. Custer's defeat at the Little Big Horn proved a pyrrhic victory for the red man. By early 1877 the Sioux and Cheyenne had been removed to reservations. Not quite a year past, Sitting Bull and his band had returned from their exile in Canada and surrendered to the army. The last of the hostiles were pacified, and the land itself opened to settlement. Most homesteaders, however, continued to pass through on their way to Oregon. The solitude and distance of the High Plains were somehow ominous. A place where few cared to try their luck.

Late the next afternoon, Starbuck topped a rise overlooking the South Fork of the Powder River. The earth shimmered under the brassy dome of the sky, and the sun seemed fixed forever on the horizon. Off in the distance the Big Horns thrust awesomely from the basin floor. A day's ride due north, deep in the foothills, lay Buffalo Creek. And somewhere beyond that, his destination. Hole-in-the-Wall.

Starbuck reined to a halt. He sat for a moment studying on the last leg of his journey. According to Nat Boswell, the ranch of Ed Houk was south of Buffalo Creek Canyon. He had no idea whether Houk was an honest man or in league with the outlaws. Either way, the rancher most certainly possessed knowledge about Hole-in-the-Wall. Any man who lived that close to the stronghold—and survived—

was a man worth knowing. A man who might be persuaded to talk. The approach would require discretion and craft; otherwise Starbuck would risk tipping his hand before he got started. Yet the odds dictated he try, for one likelihood stood out above all else. The secrets of Hole-in-the-Wall were no secret to Ed Houk.

The bay gelding suddenly alerted. He stood, nostrils flared, like an ebony statue bronzed by the sun. His hide rippled, and he nervously stamped the ground as he tested the wind. His eyes were fixed on a stand of trees bordering the river.

A visceral instinct told Starbuck to move. He never questioned such instincts; he obeyed. Too many times before some intermittent sixth sense had warned him of danger, and thereby allowed him to live awhile longer. All thought suspended, he jerked his rifle and swung down out of the saddle. A shot cracked, and in the same instant a slug fried the air around his ears. He saw a puff of smoke billow from a thicket on the riverbank.

A second slug kicked dirt at his feet as he dropped to one knee. The rifle butt slammed into his shoulder and he centered the sights on the thicket. Working the slide-action, he chambered a round and fired. Then, with no more than a pulsebeat between shots, he pumped five quick rounds into the dense undergrowth. The last report still rang in his ears when a man stumbled out of the thicket and wobbled drunkenly along the riverbank. Starbuck took careful aim and squeezed off a shot. The man's head exploded in a gory mist of brains and bone matter. He went down as though struck by a thunderbolt.

Starbuck waited several moments, scanning the

treeline. At last, satisfied the man was alone, he rose and walked down the slope. Off to one side, screened by the undergrowth, he saw a horse tied to a tree. The rifle cocked and ready, he drifted closer, approaching slowly. On the riverbank, he stopped, watchful a moment longer. He spotted a Winchester carbine on the ground behind the thicket, and grunted softly to himself. Then his gaze shifted to the body.

The man lay head down in the shallows. He was dressed in grungy range clothes and smelled of death. One of the fifty-caliber slugs had drilled him clean through, just below the breastbone. The back of his shirt, where the slug had exited, was soaked with blood. His features were no longer recognizable. The last shot had blown out his skull directly above the browline.

Starbuck searched the dead man and found no identification. Then, for a long time, he stood staring down at the body. He felt no emotion, neither anger nor remorse. He was, instead, in a state of quandary. He thought it possible that the man was a robber. One of a murderous breed who would bushwhack any stranger unfortunate enough to happen along. Yet he was no great believer in coincidence. And being jumped by two unknown men within the space of a week qualified on all counts. Which led him to the worst of all conclusions.

He'd been set up—and ambushed.

The thought jolted him into bleak awareness. Still, however deeply felt, it was tempered by uncertainty. Aside from the lawyer William Dexter, no one knew his actual destination. Nat Boswell, who was familiar with undercover work, might very well have seen through his disguise as a reporter. All the more so in light of the detailed questions he'd asked about Hole-in-the-Wall. But that presupposed a motive on the part of one or both of the men. Try as he might, he simply couldn't think of a reason why either Dexter or Boswell would have him ambushed. One thing, nonetheless, was absolutely clear. The ambush today, added to the gunfight in Cheyenne, still beggared coincidence. There was a smell about it of something planned. Or worse, something arranged.

He decided to sleep light, and watch his backtrail.

Starbuck rode into Houk's ranch late the following day. The washed blue of the plains sky grew smoky along about dusk, and lamps were already lighted in the main house. He'd timed his arrival perfectly, for there was an unwritten law on cattle spreads. A stranger was always asked to spend the night.

Ed Houk was a bony man, with shrunken skin and knobby joints. His features were seared by years of wind and sun, and his eyes were lusterless as stones. Somewhere in his early thirties, he looked older, and gave the impression of a man burned out by hard times and hard work. His outfit consisted of three hired hands and a herd of some five hundred longhorns. Whether he was a widower or simply unmarried was unclear. He volunteered little information about himself.

By the same token, he exhibited no curiosity about Starbuck. He accepted the name he was given— Arapahoe Smith—and asked no questions of a personal nature. After supper in the cook shack, he invited Starbuck up to the main house for a drink. The accommodations were sparse, and the whiskey he served was genuine popskull. Seated in cowhide chairs they sipped quietly, their talk general. Starbuck rolled himself a smoke and Houk methodically filled his pipe. After tamping down the tobacco, he struck a match and sucked the pipe to life. Then he leaned back in his chair and studied Starbuck with a look of deliberation.

"You're about to burst your britches, so go ahead and ask."

Starbuck gave him an odd smile. "Ask what?"

"About Hole-in-the-Wall."

"What gave you that idea?"

Houk took the pipe from his mouth. "There's men on the scout driftin' through here all the time."

"Who said I'm on the scout?"

"Nobody," Houk said solemnly. "Course, it don't make no nevermind to me one way or the other. I tend to my own knittin'."

Starbuck paused, looked him straight in the eye. "Suppose I was on the run?"

"Then you've got questions," Houk replied. "Everybody does, the first time they come to Hole-in-the-Wall. I just try to steer 'em in the right direction."

"Why so hospitable?"

Houk briefly explained. A code prevailed between himself and the men who haunted Hole-in-the-Wall. He watched the front door, and never gave the time of day to anyone with the look of a lawman. In return, the outlaws allowed him to live in peace and never raided his stock. The arrangement worked to the benefit of everyone involved.

"You must have a trusting nature." Starbuck casually flicked an ash off his cigarette. "How do you know I'm not a lawman?"

"Well—" Houk hesitated, took a couple of puffs

on his pipe. "First off, I ain't that bad a judge of character. You got the look about you, and I ought to know it by now. Then, there's your horse."

"What about him?"

"Boys on the dodge don't ride nothin' but the best. I never seen one yet that was a cheapskate when it come to horses. So I pegged you the minute I saw that bay gelding."

"By jingo!" Starbuck grinned, flashing his dead tooth. "Guess you got my number."

"I generally size a feller up pretty quick."

"No argument there!" Starbuck frowned, suddenly thoughtful. "A minute ago you said something about a front door?"

"Yeah?"

"I always heard there was only one door into Hole-in-the-Wall."

Houk chuckled, puffing a cloud of smoke. "You're talking about Buffalo Creek Canyon?" When Starbuck nodded, he went on. "That's whiffledust the boys spread around for lawmen. Works like a charm, too! Everybody in the whole goldang country thinks it's gospel truth."

"You mean there's more than one entrance?"

"Four altogether." Houk ticked them off on his fingers. "There's Buffalo Creek. Then there's an old Sioux trail over the Big Horns. Then there's Hole-in-the-Wall and Little Hole-in-the-Wall."

"Jeezus!" Starbuck was genuinely astounded. "I thought Buffalo Creek—the canyon—was Hole-in-the-Wall."

"Everybody does." Houk chortled slyly. "That's 'cause outsiders think the Big Horns are the 'Wall.' Ain't so, and never was."

"I don't follow you."

"Lemme draw you a map. Otherwise, I'm liable to confuse you more'n you already are."

Houk got a stub pencil and a scrap piece of paper. He began sketching with quick, bold strokes. As the map took shape, it revealed there was more to Hole-in-the-Wall than commonly thought. The hidden valley was some thirty miles in length, north to south, and roughly two miles in width. On the west, it was bounded by the Big Horns. On the east, it was bounded by towering sandstone cliffs, labeled the Red Wall. Some thirty-five miles in length, the Red Wall merged with the Big Horns in the north and the foothills in the south. The true Hole-in-the-Wall was a gap through which the Middle Fork of the Powder River flowed westward into the valley. The Little Hole-in-the-Wall was simply an ancient game trail leading eastward over the sandstone cliffs. The old Sioux trail, westward through the mountains, was nearly impassable. Buffalo Creek Canyon, the southern entrance to the valley, was by far the easiest approach. Houk penciled a number of Xs where the mouth of the canyon opened onto the valley.

"These here"—he tapped the Xs—"are the boys' cabins. Course, them are the ones that headquarter here regular. There's lots more that comes and goes as the mood suits 'em. They generally pitch camp somewheres, or hole up in a cave. All sorts of caves over here on the slope of the Big Horns."

Starbuck pondered the map a moment. "What's on the other side of the Red Wall?"

"Powder River country," Houk commented. "Whole slew of big cattle outfits over that way."

"Have they got an 'arrangement' with the boys?"

"Nope!" Houk laughed and slapped his knee. "They're fair game, all year round!"

"So they don't know about all these ways in and out of the valley?"

"Besides me, there's only one other outfit that knows."

"Oh?" Starbuck inquired evenly. "Who's that?"

"Now I'm gonna throw you for a real loop!"

Houk pointed with his pencil. He traced the path of Buffalo Creek, which flowed the length of the valley. His pencil stopped where the creek intersected the Middle Fork of the Powder. He made an X southwest of the juncture.

"That there's the Bar C spread."

"A ranch!" Starbuck stared at him, dumbfounded. "Are you saying there's an outfit in the valley itself?"

"Shore am!" Houk cackled. "Started up last summer, and they've turned it into a real nice operation. Foreman's a prince of a feller—name's Hank Devoe."

"I take it they *do* have an arrangement with the boys?"

"Live and let live," Houk said philosophically. "When you stop and think about it, the Bar C's way ahead of the game. Ain't *nobody* gonna come into that valley and try rustlin' their beeves!"

"Or yours either," Starbuck said, stringing him along. "Not while you're the boys' watchdog on the front door."

"I reckon one good turn deserves another."

Starbuck took him a step further. "Now that you mention it—you said you'd steer me in the right direction."

"Try my best," Houk said affably. "What've you got in mind?"

"You know a fellow by the name of Mike Cassidy?"

Houk slowly knocked the dottle from his pipe. "What if I do?"

"He's a friend of a friend," Starbuck lied heartily. "I was told to look him up when I got here."

"Who by . . . just exactly?"

"Somebody he'd know"—Starbuck paused for emphasis—"down at Robbers Roost."

"Tell you what—" Houk stopped, head cocked to one side. "Have a talk with Hank Devoe. If Cassidy's in the valley, Hank'll know where he's at."

Starbuck agreed, and let it drop there. With no great effort, he turned the conversation back to the valley. One question led to another, and before long he and the rancher were hunched over the map. The outcome was all he'd hoped for, and more.

Ed Houk told him all there was to know about Hole-in-the-Wall.

Chapter Seven

Oncoming summer touched the high country. At mid-day the canyon walls shimmered and the sun at its zenith seemed fixed forever in a cloudless sky. No wind stirred and the only sound was the rushing murmur of Buffalo Creek.

Starbuck halted the gelding in a patch of shade. He looped the reins around the saddlehorn and took the makings from his pocket. He creased a rolling paper, spilled tobacco from the sack, and slowly built himself a smoke. Striking a match on his thumbnail, he lit the cigarette and inhaled deeply. His gaze scanned the rocky gorge, which was narrow and winding, hemmed in by steep walls on either side. He understood now why lawmen never ventured into Hole-in-the-Wall. The canyon approach was some ten miles long, and every switchback along the snaky creek was a natural ambush site. A man soon began waiting for the crack of a rifle shot.

Some hours earlier, Starbuck had ridden out from Houk's ranch. The cattleman sent him off full of flap-jacks and good cheer, with the map tucked in his shirt pocket. A few miles northeast the rangeland petered out into a succession of hogback ridges. The terrain rose sharply thereafter, the Big Horns majestic in the early-morning sunlight. Then, suddenly, Buffalo Creek made an abrupt bend into the canyon. The plains wind dropped off into an eerie stillness; there was a sense of being entombed within the foreboding gorge. Nothing moved, and the gelding's hoofbeats echoed off the canyon walls with a ghostly clatter. Around every turn it was as though something waited, and the long ride had a telling effect. On edge and on guard, a man's nerves were soon strung wire-tight.

Gathering the reins, Starbuck nudged the bay in the ribs and rode on. He deliberately turned his mind from the canyon to the gossipy revelations of Ed Houk. Last night, with a load of rotgut under his belt, the rancher had grown talkative. Hole-in-the-Wall, according to Hank, was home to cattle rustlers and horse thieves, as well as a collection of robbers and stone-cold killers. At any given time, their number varied, for their activities took them far and wide. Still, even a conservative estimate ranged upward of fifty or more. Under one name or another, the majority were fugitives from justice, with a price on their heads. And most were determined never to be taken alive.

Contrary to popular opinion, the outlaws were not organized. Some operated in small gangs, or teamed up for a particular job. But for the most part, Hole-in-the-Wall was populated by men with a philosophy all their own. Far too independent to conform—especially to the outside world's laws and strictures—they saw no reason to impose codes on themselves within the mountain stronghold. No man was his brother's keeper, and their general attitude was a rough form of individualism that pivoted around devil take the hindmost. By choice, their lives were beset with danger, and the eternal threat of a hangman's noose. Yet, while they lived, they enjoyed a form of freedom as addictive as opium. All they needed to earn a livelihood was a fast horse and a little savvy about cows. Or a quick gun and no great conscience.

Understandably enough, Houk in no way considered himself slightly windward of the law. He saw himself and the owners of the Bar C spread as neutrals in somebody else's war. Their cattle outfits were on the fringe of civilization, and the law of might makes right prevailed. Forced to fend for themselves, they had formed an attitude toward the outlaws that was part trade-off and part accommodation. No one asked questions—or condemned the inhabitants of Hole-in-the-Wall—and no harm resulted. Whether they approved of the outlaws was beside the point, germane to nothing in the isolation of the High Plains. With no personal reason to be against the lawless element, they simply took a stand of live and let live. The badmen came and went as they pleased, and the ranchers studiously minded their own business. The trade-off was a mix of pragmatism and common sense. No one lost and everyone profited—each in his own way.

Shortly after the noon hour, Starbuck emerged from the canyon. Before him lay the valley of Hole-in-the-Wall. Some thirty miles long and two miles in breadth, the valley was split by a latticework of streams that fed into the Middle Fork of the Powder River. The streams were bordered by trees, and the valley floor resembled an emerald sea of graze. Cradled beneath high northern peaks, it was sheltered from blustery winds, and the forested mountainsides provided abundant game even in the coldest months. There was water, plenty of wood, and ample forage

for livestock. To a cattleman—or an outlaw—it
lacked for nothing.

The Red Wall, directly across the valley, rose in
a sheer thousand-foot palisade of rock. The wind-
swept battlement stretched north and south as far as
the eye could see, one great mass of vermilion-hued
sandstone. To the west, the slope of the Big Horns
climbed steadily skyward. Farther north, the mountains converged with the Red Wall, and ultimately
vanished in cloud-covered pinnacles. The green of the
valley stood out in sharp contrast between the sandstone wall and the blue-hazed mountains. There was
a smell of crystal-clear air and sweet grass. And an
almost oppressive sense of serenity.

The outlaw cabins were located where Buffalo
Creek entered the valley and made a leisurely bend
to the north. Spread out along the slope of the mountains, the cabins were constructed of logs and appeared large enough for no more than two or three
men. Starbuck counted eight buildings altogether,
each with its own log corral. There were no men in
sight, and he assumed the noonday heat had driven
them indoors. The corrals, however, gave testament
to a comment made by Ed Houk last night. Outlaws
valued their horses above all other possessions; a reliable mount often spelled the difference between life
and death. Whether bought or stolen, the animals
were selected with meticulous care. Speed and stamina were the qualities sought, and men who rode the
owlhoot considered top-notch horseflesh an investment in their trade. The horses in the corrals merely
underscored the point. There wasn't a crowbait in the
lot.

Starbuck held the bay to a walk. His inspection

of the cabins was casual, and he swung wide of the slope. Across the valley he spotted Little Hole-in-the-Wall, the old game trail, leading over the escarpment to Powder River country. From what Houk had told him, rustlers occasionally used the trail to spirit stolen livestock over the wall and into the valley. The primary entrance from the east, however, was some miles farther north. There, within the gap carved out by the Middle Fork of the Powder, was the true Hole-in-the-Wall. Horses and cattle were routinely driven through the gap from ranches in eastern Wyoming.

Once in the valley, there was little problem in hiding stolen livestock. The mountain slopes to the west were laced with hidden gullies and box canyons which made perfect holding pens. The outlaws also constructed cleverly concealed pole corrals in stands of trees along the streams. Farther up the slope, where timber was more abundant, dead trees were used to build an enclosure that resembled a blowdown. In each instance, the corrals were camouflaged and designed to fit in with the natural surroundings. The purpose, so far as Starbuck could determine, was to protect the livestock from fellow thieves. No one attempted to recover stolen stock from Hole-in-the-Wall.

Nor were the outlaws in imminent danger. The valley afforded them several natural hideouts, all of which were virtually invisible to an outsider. On the slope to the west, canyons and gullies concealed men with even greater ease than rustled livestock. Along the base of the Red Wall there were numerous caverns, with subterranean passages leading from one to the other. Anyone familiar with the layout could hide for days, perhaps months, with no fear of discovery.

Yet that, too, was a matter of small likelihood. No one was foolhardy enough to chase outlaws into the valley. Hole-in-the-Wall was a world unto itself, at once mysterious and deadly. And forever inviolate.

Ed Houk had revealed all these secrets and more last night. Starbuck was nonetheless leery; his cynicism had never betrayed him before, and a grain of salt seemed prudent where the rancher was concerned. For all his garrulous good humor, Houk hadn't been totally forthcoming. The odds dictated that he knew exactly where to locate Mike Cassidy. But he'd evaded the question by steering Starbuck to the Bar C foreman, Hank Devoe. All that led to a reasonable assumption, and reinforced the need for caution. Houk was playing for time, and fully intended to warn Mike Cassidy. Before nightfall, the outlaw would have gotten the message. A stranger was inquiring about him—by name.

Starbuck considered it a matter of spilt milk. He'd asked the question—taken a calculated risk—and there was nothing to be gained in regrets. For now, however, he'd lost the element of surprise. His next step would be determined largely by what he learned from Hank Devoe. He steeled himself to give a memorable performance for the Bar C foreman. He would underplay the role, thereby lending Arapahoe Smith a certain larger-than-life deadliness. The character of a mankiller was, after all, one he understood completely. With only minor variations, the part was very much made to order.

He would play himself.

The Bar C headquarters was impressive. Substantial log buildings within the compound included a main house, a large bunkhouse with attached cook shack, and several smaller outbuildings. Some distance beyond the bunkhouse was a log corral.

The compound was situated on a stretch of grassland ten miles north of the outlaw cabins. Easily identified, the spot was located where Buffalo Creek emptied into the Middle Fork of the Powder. Across the creek was another landmark—Steamboat Rock— a massive chunk of sandstone shaped along the lines of a paddle-wheeler. A mile or so due north of the compound, the river made a sharp turn eastward through the Red Wall. This narrow gap, formed by erosion along the riverbed, was the true Hole-in-the-Wall. The valley itself extended northward for another twelve miles beyond the compound. There the Red Wall joined the Big Horn Range.

Starbuck rode into the compound late that afternoon. By the size of the operation, he judged the Bar C would have a crew of no fewer than ten cowhands. The owners were a couple of wealthy cattlemen who seldom came anywhere near the ranch. He'd been told by Ed Houk that they lived in Cheyenne, and gave their foreman a free hand in running the outfit. If true, that made Hank Devoe a man of some stature in the valley. Operating a spread in the middle of Hole-in-the-Wall—while maintaining a neutral position toward the outlaws—would require the tact of a diplomat on foreign ground. And above all else, it would demand a tightlipped attitude toward outsiders.

Several things indicated that Devoe was no slouch at walking on thin ice. When the outlaws went east of the Red Wall, into Powder River country, their raids were generally conducted at night. Allowing time for trailing the cows westward, that meant they would pass through Hole-in-the-Wall and enter the valley somewhere after sunrise. Which, in turn, meant the stolen livestock would be driven past the Bar C headquarters in broad daylight. It followed, then, that Devoe would have firsthand knowledge of the brands on the rustled cows. From there, it required no mental genius to deduce which ranches had been raided. He would, moreover, know the names of the outlaws who had pulled the job. All in all, it was dangerous information, especially if Devoe leaked it to the wrong people. Apparently he wore blinders and possessed the ability to button his lip. Otherwise, he would have long since taken a one-way trip to the boneyard.

Starbuck dismounted outside the main house. A moment later an ox of a man stepped through the door and walked forward. He was a big, rawboned fellow, standing well over six feet, with not an ounce of suet on his frame. His jaw was stuffed with a quid of tobacco, and his eyes were impersonal. His gaze swept Starbuck's grizzled appearance, lingering an instant on the conchas belt and the crossdraw holster. Then he stopped, and nodded.

"Howdy."

"Hullo yourself." Starbuck's tone was low, slightly abrasive. "I'm looking for Hank Devoe."

"You've found him." Devoe stuck out his hand. "I don't believe I caught your name."

"Arapahoe Smith." Starbuck shook once, a hard up-and-down pump. "I was told you're the man to see at Hole-in-the-Wall."

"Who told you that?"

"Ed Houk."

"You a friend of Ed's?"

"Nope," Starbuck said bluntly. "Never set eyes on him before yesterday."

"Why'd he send you to me?"

"Mostly because he's a piss-willie."

Devoe hesitated, clearly surprised. "Ed wouldn't take kindly to anybody talkin' like that."

"I don't give a good goddamn whether he would or not."

"You might if it got back to him."

"Nothing I wouldn't say to his face."

"Suppose I told you Ed's a friend of mine?"

"That's your problem."

"And if I took exception to you callin' him names?"

"Then you've bought yourself a bigger problem."

Starbuck's manner was cold, and deadly. He'd learned early in life that confidence counted far more than the odds. A man assured of himself bred that same conviction in other men, and as a result, forever held the edge. His performance was calculated to create an impression, one that left no room for doubt. Arapahoe Smith was a man with an explosive temper and a short fuse. A killer.

Devoe's appraisal of him was deliberate. After a time, the foreman turned his head and spat a brownish squirt of tobacco juice. He watched as it hit the ground and kicked up a puff of dust. Then he looked around.

"What makes you think Ed's a piss-willie?"

"I asked him a simple question," Starbuck said flatly. "He gave me a song and dance, and passed it along to you. I got the impression he don't hardly take a leak without asking permission."

"All depends on the question." Devoe paused,

shifted the quid to the other side of his mouth. "Around here, there's some questions better left unanswered."

"I'm not one for loose talk, myself. All I want's a civil answer and no ring-around-the-rosy."

"Awright, go ahead and ask your question."

"Whereabouts would I find Mike Cassidy?"

Devoe hawked as though he'd swallowed a bone. "Judas Priest! It's no wonder Ed gave you the fast shuffle."

Starbuck's eyes took on a peculiar glitter. "I rode five hundred miles to hear the answer. So do yourself a favor, and don't hand me another dummy routine."

"Mr. Smith," Devoe said hesitantly, "if I was to talk out of school about Mike, I wouldn't last long anyway. To get answers, you got to give a few. Otherwise my lips are sewed shut."

"What'd you have in mind?"

"For openers—" Devoe stopped, met his gaze. "Who are you and where're you from?"

"I already told you." Starbuck looked annoyed. "The name's Arapahoe Smith."

"So you did," Devoe agreed. "But you left out the where from."

"Robbers Roost."

"Are you wanted?"

"I sure as hell didn't ride all the way up here for the scenery."

"What's the charge?"

"Murder." Starbuck grinned crookedly. "A fellow asked me one too many questions, and I put a leak in his ticker."

Devoe eyed him in silence a moment. "You a friend of Mike's?"

"A secondhand friend," Starbuck noted dryly. "Somebody down at Robbers Roost gave me his name."

"Why so?"

"I had to light out pretty sudden, and Hole-in-the-Wall seemed the natural place to come. He told me Cassidy was a square shooter."

"That's it?" Devoe persisted. "You're lookin' for a place to lay low—nothin' more?"

"Nothin' more?" Starbuck rocked his head from side to side. "I don't get your drift."

"Lemme say it another way," Devoe rumbled. "If you're a lawman—or you've got some personal score to settle with Mike—then I'd advise you to make dust and not look back. It's the only way you'll ever leave here alive."

"I'm no lawdog!" Starbuck bristled. "And I never even met Cassidy. So how the Christ could it be anything personal?"

"All I'm tryin' to do is warn you."

"Don't do me any favors." There was a hard edge to Starbuck's voice. "You've had your answers and now I'll have mine. Whereabouts do I find Cassidy?"

Devoe looked down and studied the ground. "I hope you're who you say you are, Mr. Arapahoe Smith. If you're not, then take my word for it—we're both dead men!"

Starbuck laughed. "I aim to live awhile yet."

"I'm mighty relieved to hear it."

"And I'm still waiting for directions."

Devoe considered a moment, then gave him a slow nod. "I take it you come in by way of Buffalo Creek Canyon?"

"You take it right."

"Head back that direction," Devoe said, motioning down the valley. "You recollect them cabins, on the west side of the creek?"

"I got pretty good eyesight."

"Try the third cabin headed south. Last time I heard, that's where Mike called home."

"He bunk alone?" Starbuck asked. "Or does he have a pardner?"

"Search me." Devoe shrugged noncommittally. "I stick to this end of the valley."

Starbuck walked to his horse. He stepped into the saddle, then his gaze settled on Devoe. His mouth quirked and he bobbed his head.

"I always remember a favor, Mr. Devoe."

"That's a comforting thought, Mr. Smith."

Starbuck chuckled and rode off down the valley.

Chapter Eight

A sky of purest indigo was flecked through with stars. On the creek bank, Starbuck stood lost beneath the shadow of the trees. His eyes searched the patchwork sky, as though some magical truth were to be found there. He found instead the tangled skein of his own thoughts.

By any assessment, the situation was a mess. Starbuck prided himself on being a realist, and there was no avoiding the fact that he'd worked himself into a corner. He was in the wrong place at the wrong time, and everyone in Hole-in-the-Wall knew he was there. Worse, he was trapped in a quagmire of his own integrity. He thought it a pretty pickle for a man in the detective business.

One source of concern was Hank Devoe. Starbuck was under no illusions about the Bar C foreman. Hardly a fool, Devoe would hedge his bet. He was concerned for his own life, and with good reason. He'd broken faith with Mike Cassidy, and the consequences were not difficult to imagine. Within Hole-in-the-Wall, such a breach would be considered the cardinal sin; and the penalty was death. His fear of the hardcase named Arapahoe Smith was a momentary thing, quickly come and gone. His fear of retribution from the outlaw quarter was deeply entrenched, an overriding imperative. By now, he would have done the sensible thing and warned Cassidy. An old and widely practiced diplomatic ploy, it was known as covering your ass. And diplomacy was Hank Devoe's game.

Upon riding away from the ranch, Starbuck's bravado had abruptly vanished. He had bullied Devoe into talking, and thereby furthered completion of his assignment. At the same time, he had compounded an already dicey situation. He now knew where to find Cassidy; but Ed Houk's warning would have alerted the outlaw. So he was expected, and his cover story would never withstand close questioning by Cassidy. To approach the cabin in daylight—without the element of surprise—was no longer an option. He'd lost the edge.

A mile or so from the ranch, Starbuck had forded Buffalo Creek. Thereafter he stuck to the treeline as he made his way down the valley. The sun was dipping westward toward the mountains when he halted opposite the outlaw cabins. He left the bay to graze, tied by a slack length of rope to a tree. Then, moving through the wooded grove, he found a vantage point where he could smoke and think without being seen. His guess was that Hank Devoe had wasted no time in getting a message to Cassidy. On top of the warning from Houk, that would make the outlaw doubly vigilant. All of which made a sorry state of affairs even sorrier.

Starbuck's original plan was a washout. As he'd done on past cases, he had thought to infiltrate a gang of outlaws by passing himself off as a man on the dodge. Once his credentials were established, he would have bided his time and awaited an opportune moment. On one pretext or another he would have then picked a fight with Cassidy and killed him. An unknown who called himself Arapahoe Smith would have been credited with the killing, and no one the wiser. At that point he would have gotten on his horse and vanished without a trace. Assignment completed.

None of that had happened for the simplest of reasons. His plan, from the very outset, was based on a false premise. There was no gang at Hole-in-the-Wall. There was, instead, a loose confederation of outlaws. Which left him with nothing to infiltrate, no way to worm his way into a collection of loners. Forced to ask too many questions too fast, he'd alarmed Ed Houk and inadvertently alerted Cassidy. The upshot was not unlike entering the valley at the head of a brass band. The thump of a bass drum and the clash of cymbals would hardly have attracted more attention. So now he had no choice but to improvise as he went along. There was no alternative plan, and no way to resurrect the original scheme. He was playing it fast and loose—one step at a time.

The immediate problem was Mike Cassidy. Not how to kill him, but rather how to kill him in an acceptable manner. Starbuck was no assassin. He believed certain men deserved to die, and he felt no twinge of conscience about hurrying them along to the grave. Yet he operated by a code that allowed him to live with himself in the aftermath. He never back-shot a man, and in all the years he'd worked his trade, he had never bushwhacked anyone. His gun was for hire, but his soul wasn't for sale. He took a wanted man from the front or not at all.

Expediency was nonetheless central to his code. A manhunter was no paladin of social conduct, and killing men was by no means a game. Only one rule existed: survive the encounter and live to fight another day. Starbuck gave the other man a chance—a very slim chance—but he gave no man the edge. His customary practice was to get the drop on an outlaw and order him to surrender. Barring that, he openly challenged a wanted man and shot him down on the spot. He killed quickly and cleanly, and without remorse.

Tonight, he would kill again in a similar fashion. His position in the trees afforded him an unobstructed view across the valley. From dusk until dark, he had watched Cassidy's cabin like a hawk zeroed on a barnyard hen. The distance was not quite a mile, and he'd had no trouble spotting the lone figure of a man. At sundown, a couple of horses in the corral had been grained and watered, and afterward the man had split some firewood. With darkness, a lamp was lighted in the cabin and a tendril of smoke drifted upward from the chimney. None of the other outlaws came near the cabin, and the sign seemed plain enough to read. Cassidy was a loner.

Starbuck saw it as an exercise in stealth. His approach to the cabin would be made quietly, without spooking the horses. Once there, he would make positive identification through the cabin window. He'd memorized Cassidy's description from his rogues' gallery, and there would be no mistake on that score. Then, with his gun drawn, he would kick in the door. The outcome was a foregone conclusion. Cassidy's instinctive reaction would be to fight, make a try for his gun. He would die trying.

Under cover of darkness, Starbuck would then make his way back to the creek. It was a tossup whether the shooting would draw the other outlaws from their cabins. They might come to investigate, or they might consider it none of their affair. Either way, it made little difference in the overall scheme of things. By that time, Starbuck planned to be well on his way downstream. He would lead the bay a mile or so into the canyon before he mounted. Then he would ride through the night and on into the next day. Arapahoe Smith would be roundly cursed at Hole-in-the-Wall. And seen no more.

Which was a fitting end to an assignment properly executed.

Satisfied it would work, Starbuck walked back through the woods. He made supper on creek water and jerky from his saddlebags. He suppressed the temptation for a cigarette, unwilling to risk the operation on the flare of a match. Later, when the job was done, would be time enough. He watered the bay at the creek, and afterward snubbed him tight to a tree. Then he turned and moved swiftly into the pale starlight.

He drifted across the valley quiet as woodsmoke.

Starbuck crept along an arroyo that snaked westward behind the cabin. Some thirty yards away, he halted and slowly surveyed the corral. He was alert to any sound, any telltale indication the horses had winded him or sensed his presence. The animals stood hipshot in the silty starlight. He quit the shadows and scrambled out of the defile.

Skirting the corral, he catfooted across the open ground. At the rear of the cabin, he stopped and let his heartbeat slow. Then, icy calm restored, he peered cautiously around the corner. A cider glow filtered through the window, casting puddled light on the earth. A few steps farther on was the door. He heard nothing, and he quickly scanned other cabins in the near distance. There was no one in sight.

Stepping around the corner, he flattened himself against the wall and inched toward the spill of light. He removed his hat and eased to a halt beside the window. Then, with the utmost care, he edged one eye around the casement. He burned every detail of the room into his mind.

The cabin was crude as a wolf's den. A rough-hewn table, with a couple of homemade chairs, occupied the center of the room. Skillets and cast-iron pots were scattered randomly beside an open fireplace. In the corner was a washstand, and directly above it were shelves stacked with tinned goods. Along the far wall, wedged into a corner, was a double bunk. On the upper bunk was a bare mattress; the lower bunk was covered with rumpled blankets and a single pillow. The wall nearby was draped with clothes hung on pegs; saddles and a motley collection of gear were piled on the floor. The right front wall, immediately beside the entrance, was not visible. The window angle created a blind spot from the door to the far corner. A lamp on the table bathed the whole room in flickering shadows.

There was a man seated at the table. He held a deck of cards and spread out before him was a hand of solitaire. He was swarthy, with splayed features and dark hair and a drooping mustache. Heavily muscled, with a thick neck and powerful shoulders, he had the look of a bruiser. His eyes appeared yellow, almost amber, in the lamplight. A jagged scar traced the line of his jawbone.

The man and the rogues' gallery description were

a perfect match. His name was Mike Cassidy.

Starbuck jammed on his hat and pulled the Colt. Stooping low, he ducked under the window and moved to the door. He drew a deep breath and gently thumbed back the hammer on the sixgun. Then he aimed a savage kick at the latch. The door burst open and slammed inward with a splintering groan. He charged through and halted just inside the room. His arm leveled, the Colt steady as a rock.

"You're under arrest, Cassidy!"

Cassidy took the news with unshaken aplomb. He riffled three cards off the top of the deck and laid a red nine on a black ten. Then he looked up and smiled.

"Evenin'," he said almost idly. "Been expectin' you."

"You heard me!" Starbuck pressed him. "You're wanted in Utah—on a hanging charge!"

"Hanging!" Cassidy repeated, amused. "Damned if that don't beat all."

"You got a choice," Starbuck said tightly. "Come along peaceable or I'll shoot you where you sit!"

"Wanna bet?"

A doubt suddenly struck Starbuck deep in the pit of his stomach. Something was wrong here, all ass-backwards to what he'd expected. He felt a strong misgiving about killing the man in coldblood. Yet Cassidy seemed to be inviting death.

"One last warning!" he said harshly. "On your feet or you're a dead man!"

Cassidy gave him a strange grin. "Take a look behind you, Mr. Smith. You're liable to change your mind."

"Forget the tricks and do like I say!"

"It's no trick." Cassidy glanced past him, and nodded. "Tell the man, Butch."

"Drop it! Pronto!"

Starbuck went stock-still. The voice was very close, and he realized someone had been hidden behind the door. Understanding flooded over him as though his ears had come unplugged. He's been suckered into a trap!

"I ain't gonna tell you again, mister!"

The voice was sharp, commanding. With great care, Starbuck lowered the hammer on his sixgun and dropped it. Cassidy threw back his head and roared with laughter. Then he kicked his chair aside and moved around the table.

"You got balls," he said, halting a pace away. "Yessir, you shorely do! I about halfway thought you wouldn't show."

"Guess you got the word," Starbuck said, not asking a question. "Houk and Devoe make pretty fair messenger boys."

"Yeah, they do," Cassidy admitted readily. "Course, I wouldn't't've been caught with my drawers down no-how. I knowed you was comin' long before you got here."

"You—!"

"Shut your trap!" Cassidy's mood suddenly turned sullen. "You just speak when you're spoke to! Savvy?"

"Whatever you say."

"Awright, let's start with something simple. Like, for instance . . . what's your name?"

"Arapahoe Smith."

"Don't be a wiseass," Cassidy growled. "Your real name?"

"Arapahoe Smith."

"You're not listenin'!" Cassidy jabbed a finger into his chest. "We'll try another one. Who d'you work for?"

"The law," Starbuck lied with a straight face. "I'm a U.S. deputy marshal."

"Horseshit!" Cassidy exploded. "Who hired you? Who sent you here?"

"The U.S. marshal, Utah Territory."

Cassidy's face mottled with anger. His gaze shifted to whoever stood beside the door. Starbuck saw the look, caught an undercurrent of something unspoken, and suddenly understood. He braced himself too late.

A pistol barrel cracked him across the skull. His eyes spun out of focus and pinwheels of light flashed through his head. Then Cassidy stepped forward and buried a gnarled fist in his stomach. His mouth popped open in a roaring whoosh of breath and he folded at the waist. Cassidy punched him in the jaw and he went down as though he'd been poleaxed. The whole right side of his head turned numb, and the brassy taste of blood filled his mouth. He gasped for air, his lungs on fire.

Cassidy dropped to one knee, grabbed a handful of hair. "Gimme the straight dope or you're gonna get more of the same! Who hired you?"

"Nobody."

Lifting his head, Cassidy drove a hard chopping right into his mouth. "What's your name?"

"Arapahoe—"

A paralyzing blow split his eyebrow. "Who sent you here?"

"I told—"

"You ain't told me nothin'!" Cassidy shouted. "Now smarten up and let's hear it!"

Starbuck shook his head like a man who had walked into cobwebs. His vision was muzzy and showery spots leaped before his eyes. Blood oozed down over his cheekbone and an ugly cut split his upper lip. His mouth moved, the words fragmented.

"Go . . . to . . . hell . . ."

Wordlessly, with a sort of methodical stoicism, Cassidy resumed the beating. The blows were measured and brutal, delivered with cold ferocity, like a butcher working over a side of beef. When he finished, Starbuck's face was a bloody mask, no longer a handsome sight. Cassidy still gripped a handful of hair, and he wrenched Starbuck's head back with a vicious twist. Then he leaned forward, eyeball to eyeball.

"One last time"—his mouth zigzagged in a cruel grimace—"who hired you?"

There was a moment of leaden silence. Starbuck's eyes were glazed, and he retched, spitting blood. He swallowed and gagged, and coughed a wad of bright reddish phlegm. At last he groaned, slowly regained his senses, and tried to focus through swollen eyelids. A crazed smile touched his lips and froth bubbled at the corner of his mouth.

"Kiss my ass."

Cassidy stared at him with stunned disbelief. Then his eyes flashed and his expression turned murderous. He pulled a Colt forty-four from the holster on his hip and eared the hammer to full-cock. Then he pressed the snout of the pistol against Starbuck's temple. His finger tightened on the trigger.

"Talk!" His voice was wild, homicidal. "Talk or I'll blow your head off."

Chapter Nine

A sinister stillness settled over the cabin. For a time neither of the men moved, and between them there was a sense of suppressed violence. Cassidy's eyes were hard and feral, and he stared down the gun barrel with a look of cold menace. At last, with a savage oath, he dropped Starbuck on the floor.

"Stupid sonovabitch!"

Staring down a moment, he suddenly turned and walked away. He lowered the hammer on his pistol and shoved it into the holster. His face was ocherous and he moved to the washstand, where he snatched a whiskey bottle from the overhead shelves. He pulled the cork and took a long swig, shuddering as the liquor hit bottom. Then he stalked to the table and lowered himself heavily into a chair. His expression was black and angry bafflement.

Starbuck felt dazed, punchy. His head buzzed and the room seemed to swirl in a dizzying motion. He ached all over, as though he'd been run through an ore crusher and torn apart. He levered himself up on one elbow and blinked several times, struggling to clear his head. From some distant corner of his mind, a thought surfaced and swam forward through a murky haze. He groped with it a moment, muddled and confused; then there was a slow dawning. Still, his mind was dull and sluggish, and he couldn't quite comprehend what seemed a vital enigma. He wondered why Cassidy hadn't killed him.

A hand scooped his sixgun off the floor. He glanced up and saw a young boy, somewhere in his middle teens. The youngster was of medium height and slim build, with a blunt pug nose and a square jaw. His hair was like a shock of wheat, and an unruly cowlick spilled down over his forehead. He wore rough work clothes and mule-eared boots, and a long-barreled Colt Peacemaker was strapped on his hip. Yet there was laughter in his eyes and a clownish smile, something of the prankster. He looked at once full-grown and still very much a kid.

The youngster stuffed the sixgun in the waistband of his trousers and backed away. He kept one eye on Starbuck, but his attention was clearly directed to Cassidy. He moved to the table and straddled a chair. His face clouded with a thoughtful frown, almost like a child toying with some new and inexplicable riddle. He sat watching the older man for a time. Then he hunched forward, elbows locked over the top of the chair. His voice was husky, surprisingly deep.

"Mike?"

"What?"

"You gonna bite my head off if I ask you something?"

"How'll I know till you ask?"

"Well . . ." A beat of hesitation, then he rushed on. "What stopped you? Holy moly, I figured you was gonna kill him deader'n a doornail!"

"I come goddam close!" Cassidy's eyes blazed. "I never wanted to kill nobody so bad in my whole life!"

"Then why'd you let him off?"

"Aww hell, Butch!" Cassidy grunted sharply. "I couldn't kill him! Don't you see that would've spoilt any chance I got?"

"Any chance for what?"

"Lookee here," Cassidy explained with weary patience. "Somebody hired him, didn't they? Somebody paid him blood money and sent him here to stop my clock. Am I right or not?"

"Yeah," Butch said eagerly. "And—?"

"So he's a hired gun, plain and simple!"

"All the more reason to kill him."

"No, you dope!" Cassidy took a slug from the whiskey bottle, wiped his mouth. "How'll I know who hired him lessen he talks?"

"Oooo!" Butch's mouth ovaled in wonder. "Dead men tell no tales—right?"

"On the button," Cassidy acknowledged. "Wasn't for that, I would've shot him the minute he come through the door."

"Only one trouble, Mike."

"What's that?"

"How you gonna make him talk?"

"What d'you mean?"

"Well, look at him!" Butch jerked a thumb over his shoulder. "Cripes sake! What more could you do?"

"Bastard's tough, awright." Cassidy laughed without humor. "I've whipped lots of men, but I never saw one take that kind of punishment. Did you hear him? Told me to kiss his ass!"

"Guess you gotta admire his sand."

"Either that or he's dumber'n a dog turd."

"Whichever, it's six of one and half a dozen of another."

"How so?"

"You still gotta figure a way to make him talk."

"Ain't it a fact?" Cassidy spat on his large-knuckled hands and rubbed them together. "Maybe I'll try a little Injun torture. That'd cure his lockjaw—real quick!"

"Wooiee!" Butch grinned, his teeth flashing like rows of dice. "You never told me you knowed anything about Injun torture!"

"A trick or two." Cassidy gave him a catlike smile. "Come to think of it, I reckon it'd be plumb fittin'."

"I don't get you."

"Arapahoe Smith!" Cassidy jeered. "Anybody that takes a dog-eater's name ought to be treated like one!"

"Now that you mention it," Butch wondered aloud, "what made you think that wasn't his real name?"

"Simple!" Cassidy snorted. "A hired gun wouldn't use his own handle at Hole-in-the-Wall."

"Why not?"

" 'Cause it'd be like signin' his own death warrant. Oncet word got around, he wouldn't live ten minutes! Somebody would kill him figgerin' he was out to kill them."

"Maybe." Butch puzzled on it a moment. "Or maybe he's what he says he is . . . a lawman."

"Possible," Cassidy conceded grudgingly. "I'd tend to doubt it, though."

"Well, he sure as the devil had his facts straight. All that stuff about Utah and you being wanted on a hanging charge. How do you explain that?"

"I dunno." Cassidy looked bemused. "Tell you the truth, the whole goddamn thing don't make no rhyme nor reason."

"Say he was a marshal." Butch leaned forward, earnest. "Seems to me that'd spell it out in spades. It's only natural the law would come after you sooner or later."

"Nope, it won't wash!" Cassidy announced hotly. "There ain't a lawdog alive that'd poke his nose into Hole-in-the-Wall. We got 'em buffaloed—the whole kit-'n'-caboodle—and that's gospel fact!"

"Yeah, but you said it yourself. Nobody ever took that kind of beating and kept his mouth wired shut. Maybe he's one lawman who don't scare so easy."

"He's a hired gun!" Cassidy spat angrily. "Don't make no nevermind what he says. He come here to kill me—and that's that!"

Butch's eyes skittered away, then he cleared his throat. "So what do we do now?"

"I ain't sure," Cassidy noted bitterly. "His kind are a dime a dozen, cheaper'n dirt! There'll be another one after him and then another one and another one. Once it starts, it don't end."

"What don't end?"

"Somebody wants me dead!" Cassidy's face congealed into a scowl. "I gotta learn that somebody's name and personally arrange his funeral. Otherwise, he'll keep on sendin' hired guns till one of 'em gets the job done."

"No doubt about it," Butch agreed. "Somebody aims to put you six feet under."

"Only one salvation to the whole thing. Somebody else *don't* want me dead. Except for him, I'd be pushin' up daisies right now!"

"Wonder who he is?"

"Wisht to hell I knew." Cassidy paused, mulling it over. "Anybody that sends you a warnin', the least he could do is leave his name."

"Queer the way that come about. You'd think somebody—Davis or one of the girls—would remember who dropped the word."

"Ain't it the goddamn truth!" Cassidy rasped. "Beats me how he waltzed in there and spoke his piece, and not one solitary soul recollects nothin' about him. I mean, it ain't every day some jasper leaves word one of your friends is about to get his ticket punched." He shook his head, eyes rimmed with disgust. "I can't even figger why he left a warnin'! Who the hell do I know that'd go out of his way to save my bacon?"

"Vicey versy too," Butch added quickly. "Who does he know that wants your bacon smoked?"

"If we knew that," Cassidy grumbled, "we wouldn't be sittin' here scratchin' our heads. We'd have the name of whoever it was that sent some butthole up here to shoot me!"

"You called it right, Cassidy—a butthole!"

Cassidy and Butch jumped. Starbuck was propped up on his elbow, watching them. He'd listened, slowly recovering his senses, throughout the entire conversation. He was battered but alert, and now he eased himself into a sitting position. He fixed Cassidy with a questioning look.

"All right if I get on my feet?"

"I think I like you better on the floor."

"Don't blame you." Starbuck gave him a ghastly

smile. "Only I don't talk so good on my backsides."

"Talk?" Cassidy regarded him with wary hostility. "What do you wanna talk about, just exactly?"

"The man who hired me."

A fleeting look of puzzlement crossed Cassidy's face; then his expression became flat and guarded. "Why the sudden change of heart?"

"I got an earful of what you were saying."

"Yeah?" Cassidy eyed him suspiciously. "So?"

"A little bird tells me we've been played for saps."

"You'll have to spell it out plainer'n that."

"We were set up!" Starbuck said fiercely. "Everything that happened here tonight was rigged to get us both killed!"

Cassidy and Butch exchanged a baffled look. Then the outlaw's gaze swung back to Starbuck. His face was pinched in an oxlike frown.

"You're gonna be in a helluva fix if you ain't able to make that stick."

"Won't hurt you to listen."

"Why not, Mike?" Butch interjected. "He might just know something we don't!"

"Well . . ." Cassidy hesitated, then nodded to Starbuck. "None of your monkeyshines! You try anything funny and I'll put your lights out."

"I've got nothing up my sleeve."

"Slow and easy does it," Cassidy said, motioning. "Butch, let him have your chair. You come on around here with me."

Butch obediently rose and circled the table. He stopped beside Cassidy, his hand resting on the butt of his pistol. Then, watchful and alert, they waited.

Starbuck took a tight grip on himself. He climbed

unsteadily to his feet and stood for a moment, rocked by a wave of dizziness. He was aware Cassidy might yet kill him. Still, there was strong indication that someone was manipulating them like puppets on a string. He'd decided to level with the outlaw, and take his chances. The time for guile and subterfuge was past.

Some moments elapsed before his head cleared. Finally, he walked to the chair and sat down. He pulled a handkerchief from his hip pocket and gingerly dabbed the cuts on his lip and brow. His left eye was swollen almost completely shut, and he thought it entirely likely his nose was broken. The handkerchief stemmed the flow of blood, and at last he realized he could stall no longer. It was time now to talk for his life.

"You weren't far off," he said, staring across the table at Cassidy. "The name's Luke Starbuck. I'm a detective, working out of Denver."

"I've heard the name." Cassidy fixed him with an evil look. "You've got yourself quite a reputation as a man-killer."

"No argument there," Starbuck said slowly. "No apology, either. It's part of the detective business."

"And you were sent here to kill me—weren't you?"

"Yeah, I was," Starbuck nodded soberly. "The price was ten thousand dollars and no questions asked."

"Ten—" Cassidy glowered at him with pop-eyed amazement. "Christ on a crutch! Somebody wanted me dead real bad."

"Unless I'm wrong, the whole scheme was cooked up to get me. You were just a bonus prize."

"Scheme?" Cassidy repeated blankly. "What d'you mean by that?"

Starbuck briefly explained. He related the gist of his meeting with the lawyer William Dexter. He next detailed the reason behind the assignment—robbery of the Butte mining company—and the client's name, Ira Lloyd. Then he recounted the gunfight in Cheyenne and the ambush on the trail to Hole-in-the-Wall. He saw now that neither of those incidents was happenstance. He'd been waylaid both times, and tonight was merely a last-ditch effort in an elaborate assassination plot. Somebody had sandbagged the odds to make triple certain he would wind up dead. And that somebody's name was Ira Lloyd.

"In other words," Starbuck concluded, "he figured if his own boys missed, then you'd get me. That's why you were warned I was on my way to Hole-in-the-Wall. He wanted you primed and ready to shoot the minute a stranger asked your name."

"Maybe." Cassidy examined the notion. "Leastways it'd explain why I got the warnin' so roundabout."

"I heard Butch mention Davis and the girls. Who's Davis?"

"Al Davis," Butch said with a wide, peg-toothed grin. "He owns the saloon and cathouse down at Cheever's Flats."

"What's Cheever's Flats?"

"A tradin' post," Butch replied. "North of Ed Houk's place, about a day's ride."

"Exactly what kind of warning was it?"

"Cut and dried," Cassidy informed him. "The fella said a hired gun was gonna settle my hash."

"No explanation?"

"None a-tall."

"Well, the reason's pretty clear now."

"Yeah?" Cassidy said shortly. "Like what?"

"Vengeance." Starbuck rocked his hand, fingers splayed. "Or maybe double vengeance. Lloyd probably figured we'd kill each other."

"Don't make no sense!" Cassidy gave him a baleful look. "I never been to Butte and I never pulled no payroll job. And I damn sure don't know nobody named Ira Lloyd!"

"All the same," Starbuck insisted, "there has to be a link, something that connects us together. Lloyd didn't just pull our names out of a hat."

"What link?" Cassidy crowed. "You and me ain't exactly got a lot in common!"

"Maybe." Starbuck rubbed his chin, thoughtful. "Maybe not."

"No maybe about it! You're upwind of the law and I'm downwind. Where's the connection?"

"Well, in a manner of speaking, we both wallow at the same mud hole."

"You just lost me."

"Look at it this way," Starbuck suggested. "It's possible we know some of the same people. Don't forget, I spend a lot of time with men in your . . . line of work."

"Then how come we never crossed paths before?"

"I didn't say that," Starbuck corrected him. "I'm talking about an indirect link. Somebody we both had dealings with at one time or another."

"Hmmm." Cassidy considered a moment. "You mean somebody I might've rode with?"

"That wouldn't be a bad place to start."

"Won't take long, either," Cassidy observed. "Not countin' Butch, I've only had two partners in my whole life. One was Latigo Spence. We worked together close to four years down in Utah. The other was Dutch Henry Horn. We used to steal horses and pull a few holdups, mostly in Texas."

A strange light came into Starbuck's eyes. "When was that?"

Cassidy's brow seamed in concentration. "Near as I recollect, we busted up the summer of '75. We had a fallin' out—bastard wouldn't divvy the split proper—and I winged him."

"You shot him?"

"Damn right!" Cassidy trumpeted. "He pulled a gun on me!"

"What happened then?"

"Nothin' much." Cassidy shrugged, remembering. "I went on to Utah and started workin' out of Robbers Roost." He paused, suddenly aware of Starbuck's expression. "Why all the questions about Horn?"

"Because he's our link."

"How so?"

"I killed Dutch Henry the summer of '76."

Starbuck quickly related the story. On his first job as a range detective, he'd been hired to track down a gang of horse thieves. Some months later, at a desolate spot in No-Man's-Land, the gang had been wiped out by a posse of ranchers and cowhands. The leader escaped, however, and Starbuck had trailed him to Colorado. There, in the town of Pueblo, the chase had finally ended. Starbuck killed Dutch Henry in a gunfight.

For a long while no one spoke. Cassidy stared down at the table, and Starbuck gazed off into space with the look of a man who had stumbled upon an unexpected revelation. Then, with a coarse grunt, Cassidy shook his head.

"So we both knew Dutch Henry? What's that got to do with anything?"

"It's a link." Starbuck regarded him with a level gaze. "Unless I miss my guess, it's the only link."

Their eyes locked, and after a moment Cassidy slowly nodded. "You figgerin' what I think you're figgerin'?"

Starbuck cracked a smile. "I wouldn't be surprised."

"You're gonna pay this Ira Lloyd a visit?"

"I'd say it's time . . . way past time."

Chapter Ten

A dingy haze lighted the sky at false dawn.

Cassidy and Starbuck stepped from the cabin and stood talking quietly. Between them was the unspoken respect of one hard man for another. There was nothing akin to friendship, and under different circumstances each would have killed the other without a moment's hesitation. Only a common danger united them, and it was more a mutual pact than a bond. Today they were allies.

Starbuck's features were puffy and discolored. Several hours' sleep had restored his vitality, but the shellacking he'd taken was certain to leave scars. He looked vaguely as if he'd had his face shoved into a meat-grinder. His nose was now crooked at a slight angle and his left eye was a kaleidoscope of black and blue. His eyebrow was caked with dried blood, as was the scabbed-over cut on his bottom lip. For all that, he nonetheless thought himself the luckiest of men. He was still alive.

Last night his position had been touch and go for a long while. Even though Cassidy bought his story, the undercurrent of hostility hadn't entirely disappeared. He sensed his life was forfeit at any moment; Cassidy's normal reaction would have been to kill him and personally settle the score with Ira Lloyd.

Neither of them was comfortable with the thought of another man doing their killing. Yet he'd argued far into the night that he was the natural choice for the job. Cassidy was known—and wanted—fair game outside Hole-in-the-Wall. Starbuck, on the other hand, was at liberty to move about at will. He was, moreover, the man with the larger grievance. The whole scheme had been rigged with his death in mind. That gave him first rights—prior claim.

With some reluctance, Cassidy had finally agreed. He was by no means content with the arrangement; but he felt Starbuck's argument had merit. Fair was fair, and the one with the bigger bone to pick was the one who deserved a crack at the job. Then, too, he was something of a realist himself, and willing to give credit where credit was due. Starbuck was the more experienced mankiller, and experience counted. All the signs thus far underscored what seemed an indisputable point. Killing Ira Lloyd would be no simple chore.

The bargain struck, they'd left it there. Starbuck's sixgun was returned, and he'd been offered a bunk for the night. Butch was sent to fetch his horse from the creek, and Cassidy went back to his bottle. Before drifting off to sleep, Starbuck had decided the new alliance would stand only so much strain. He intended to start the hunt at Cheever's Flats, and it was a point he'd neglected to mention. He had no idea whether Cassidy would object, but he wanted no more words, no further argument. He wanted to be gone from Hole-in-the-Wall. And the sooner the better.

Standing now with Cassidy, his attention was drawn to the corral. Butch had the bay gelding saddled, and was leading him through the gate. Starbuck was intrigued, his curiosity aroused. The youngster was happy-go-lucky, with a sunny disposition and no evidence of a mean streak. He was the exact opposite of Cassidy, and seemed an unlikely outlaw, aspiring or otherwise. For partners, the man and the kid were an odd match, hardly birds of a feather. It was something to ponder.

Butch walked the gelding to the front of the cabin. He stopped and handed the reins to Starbuck. Then he grinned with brash impudence.

"You stick around"—he ducked his head at the bay—"and somebody's liable to steal him out from under you."

Starbuck smiled. "That somebody's name wouldn't be . . ." His voice trailed off, and he cocked his head to one side. "I guess I never thought to ask. What is your name, anyway?"

"Cassidy!" Butch swelled with pride. "Same as Mike's!"

"You two related?"

"Naw!" Butch's grin widened. "Lots of folks think that 'cause of us being partners. We're not kin, though. I just took Mike's name when we teamed up."

"How'd you get together?"

"Blind luck," Butch confessed. "I got in a little scrape and lit out for Robbers Roost. Mike took me in and taught me the business. Owe it all to him!"

"Quit braggin'," Cassidy ribbed him. "You ain't no great shakes as a horse thief . . . not yet."

"Says you!" Butch laughed. "I got the natural touch—born to it!"

"What you got," Cassidy said with grumpy good humor, "is a gift for gab." He paused, glanced at Starbuck. "Never knowed a squirt to toot his own horn so much."

"From what I hear," Starbuck said wryly, "he's got a good teacher. Your wanted dodger's still plastered all over Utah."

"Now that you mention it"—Cassidy squinted at him—"that brings us around to some unfinished business."

"What's that?"

"You being a lawman." Cassidy looked uncomfortable. "Or leastways a detective."

A vein pulsed in Starbuck's forehead. "So?"

"Well, first off, lemme say I ain't too proud of the way I roughed you up last night. Except for Butch crackin' you on the head, you'd've probably dished out as good as you got."

Starbuck brushed away the apology. "I reckon you had cause. In your position, I would have done the same—or worse."

"I come close to that, too."

"So I remember."

Cassidy paused, regarding him with a dour look. "I let you off the hook, and I'd like a favor in return."

"Unfinished business means you're calling the marker?"

"Guess it does," Cassidy said, deadly earnest. "I want your word you'll keep what you learned about Hole-in-the-Wall to yourself."

Starbuck stared at him a long time, finally drew a deep breath. "You ask a lot."

"No more'n I gave," Cassidy said grimly. "Would've been lots easier to send you up the flume and end it permanent."

A moment passed, then Starbuck shrugged. "All right, you've got my word."

"That's good enough for me."

"How'd you know I would go along?"

"I didn't." Cassidy's eyes burned with intensity. " 'Course, without your word, you wouldn't never have made it through the canyon." He gestured toward the other cabins. "Some of the boys would've dry-gulched you."

Starbuck nodded, digesting the thought. "What's to stop them from doing it anyhow?"

"A handshake." Cassidy extended his hand. "That's the signal we've come to an understandin'."

Starbuck pumped his arm vigorously. "Let's make sure they get the message."

"Don't trouble yourself." A slow smile spread over Cassidy's face. "You're in the clear . . . now."

"We're square, then." Starbuck forcefully stressed the point. "The marker's paid in full."

Cassidy made a small nod of acknowledgment. "You don't owe me nothin'."

"I'll remember that," Starbuck said quietly, "if we ever meet again."

"Hope we don't!" Cassidy suddenly chuckled. "Got an idea it'd wind up a double funeral!"

"No argument there, Mike."

Starbuck waved to Butch and swung aboard the gelding. He rode toward the creek, aware he was being closely scrutinized by men in the other cabins. The first rays of sunrise broke over the sandstone ramparts as he turned into the canyon. He gigged the bay and left Hole-in-the-Wall behind him.

· · ·

All the way through the canyon Starbuck examined various possibilities. He mentally rehashed what he'd uncovered and played the devil's advocate with himself. He arrived at only one conclusion.

For a detective, he was the prize bonehead of all time. He'd outsmarted himself, and he had underestimated everyone involved in the case. Worse, he had violated the supreme rule by which a manhunter lived. He'd let them do it to him—not the other way around.

There was no denying the facts. It all fit together like a template, events dovetailed one to the other with unquestionable timing. Despite himself, he had to admit he'd been gaffed by William Dexter. He had swallowed the lawyer's story—bait and all—leaping at the challenge of infiltrating Hole-in-the-Wall. Then, with his judgment already clouded, he had ignored one coincidence after another. He was cocky and overconfident, and only from the vantage point of hindsight had he paused to evaluate the situation. That lapse had almost gotten him killed.

Now, with a grudging sense of realization, he knew he couldn't afford another mistake. He had no idea why Ira Lloyd wanted him dead. He hadn't the faintest clue to the mine owner's connection with Dutch Henry Horn. A connection out of the past, moldering with age and the unmistakable smell of revenge. Yet one thing was very certain. Ira Lloyd was slippery and shrewd, and possessed an absolute genius for treachery. Not a man to be taken lightly, or allowed an even break. The game was dirty pool, no rules and winner take all. The loser got buried.

Late that morning, Starbuck emerged from the canyon onto the plains. His thoughts were hardened around indrawn resolve. He was determined to regain the edge, and force the fight on ground of his own choosing. Then he would kill the man who had tried to kill him.

He rode north into the Big Horn Basin.

Cheever's Flats was a crude collection of three buildings. A trading post, owned by John Cheever, stocked supplies for ranchers and outlaws and those traveling the old Bridger Trail. Next door was a blacksmith shop, and across the way was what people charitably termed a road ranch.

A combination saloon and whorehouse, the establishment was operated by Al Davis. His customers were only slightly rougher than his girls, and he considered himself a High Plains entrepreneur. He sold snakehead whiskey and rented his soiled doves by the trick or by the hour.

The last streamers of light dipped below the horizon as Starbuck rode into Cheever's Flats. Then the sky turned dusky mauve and the buildings suddenly lay cloaked in shadow. He angled across to the road ranch and stepped from the saddle. Tying the bay to a hitch rack, he walked directly to the door and banged it open. He entered with a bluff air of assurance.

The interior was dimly lighted and silent as a tomb. A pair of harridans, both of them ugly as sin, had a table staked out at the rear of the room. Neither of the girls appeared anxious for business, and they scarcely glanced at him as he stepped inside the door. On the opposite wall was a plank bar, and a lone customer stood bellied up to the counter. The barkeep was heavyset, with a ginger-colored walrus mustache and a mail-order toupee. He looked like an over-stuffed Kewpie doll with tusks.

Starbuck crossed to the bar. He picked a spot at the far end of the counter, away from the solitary drinker. The barkeep ambled over, and he nodded. "Whiskey."

"Dollar a shot, friend."

"I didn't ask the price," Starbuck said curtly. "Just bring me a bottle and a glass."

"Suit yourself."

"I generally do."

While he waited, Starbuck rolled a smoke. He struck a match on the counter and lit up, inhaling a long drag. The barkeep returned with a bottle and glass, and poured. He blew smoke in the fat man's face.

"You Al Davis?"

"I was the last time I checked."

"Keep it short and simple," Starbuck ordered. "I ain't here to be entertained."

"No offense." Davis' voice was phlegmy, with the hoarse rasp of a boozer. "What can I do for you?"

"Mike Cassidy sent me." Starbuck blew a perfect smoke ring toward the ceiling. Then, waiting for it to widen, he puffed a smaller one straight through the center. "You're gonna gimme some information Mike wants. He said to tell you he'd count it a personal favor."

Davis gave him a blank stare. "What sort of information?"

"A week or so back," Starbuck said stolidly,

"somebody wandered in here and left a warnin' for Mike. You recall that, don't you?"

"I—" Davis' face went pale, and he couldn't seem to keep his hands still. "Why do you ask?"

"You told Mike you couldn't remember the jasper or what he looked like."

"No, I didn't either," Davis protested. "I told Mike I never knew who said it."

"Then that makes you an even bigger liar."

"Wait a minute!" Davis said indignantly. "You got no right to come in here and start calling me names!"

Starbuck's smile seemed frozen. "I'll call you dog and you'll wag your tail! 'Cause if you don't, I'll kick your lardass right up between your shoulders. You begin to get the picture?"

Davis' eyes went round as saucers. "I think I got it."

"You're smarter'n you look." Starbuck studied his downcast face a moment. "Now, we'll make this quick and painless. I want a description of whoever it was that left the warnin'."

"Description?"

"You ain't deaf, are you?"

"No." Davis averted his eyes, darted a quick glance along the bar. "I don't know as I could do that."

Starbuck got the uncanny impression he was being told something without words. He leaned into the counter, motioned Davis closer. "You afraid to talk?"

"Yessir, I am," Davis said in a hoarse whisper. "Mortally afraid."

"Why so?"

"That's him!" Davis hissed. "The one at the end of the bar!"

"You're sure?" Starbuck demanded. "No mistake?"

"None," Davis muttered softly. "He come in not ten minutes ago. Asked me if I'd had any news from Hole-in-the-Wall."

"How come you suddenly remembered him?"

"Just did," Davis said weakly. "When he asked me that, I placed his face from last time."

"If you're lyin'," Starbuck growled, "I'm gonna turn your blubber into worm meat."

"Honest to Christ, I'm telling you! It's him!"

Starbuck was still leaning on the bar. He casually dropped his hand below the counter and eased it inside his vest. His fingers closed around the butt of the Colt and he slipped it from the crossdraw holster. Then he turned his head just far enough to rivet the man with a look.

"Mister, I'd like a word with you."

The man was unremarkable in appearance. He wore soiled range clothes and a battered slouch hat. He was of average height, trimly built, with the kind of face lost in a crowd. The only thing noteworthy was the pistol positioned close to hand. It looked well oiled, and much used. He straightened slightly, then turned. His gaze settled on Starbuck.

"You talking to me?"

"Nobody else," Starbuck said with a wintry smile. "I understand you've been askin' questions about Hole-in-the-Wall?"

"What's that to you?"

"All depends."

"On what?"

"On who you know at Hole-in-the-Wall."

"Try me and see."

"How about Mike Cassidy?"

"Never heard of him."

"You're plumb certain?"

"Positive."

"Then how come you're back here checkin' on things?"

"What things?"

"The warnin' you left Cassidy . . . about me?"

"Hold off a—"

The gun appeared in the man's hand and he fired a hurried snap shot. The slug plowed a furrow in the counter at Starbuck's elbow. He shifted, swinging the Colt from beneath his vest, and touched off the trigger. The pistol roared, spat a sheet of flame.

A surprised look came over the man's face. He dropped the gun and raised both arms, like a preacher warding off evil spirits. Then a splotch of red widened across his chest and his legs went rubbery. He sat down heavily on the floor.

Starbuck approached and knelt beside him. "You're dead, so it don't matter now. Tell me about Ira Lloyd."

"Who's he?"

"The man who hired you to kill me."

"That's a . . . laugh."

"Quit stalling!" Starbuck commanded. "You don't owe Lloyd nothing. Spill it while you got time!"

"Nothing . . . to . . . say."

"C'mon, talk! What've you got to lose?"

"Starbuck"—the man smiled and a trickle of blood leaked out of his mouth—"you fool."

His grin became a wet chuckle, then a strangled

cough. Suddenly he choked and vomited a great gout of blood down across his shirtfront. His eyeballs rolled back in his head and he dropped dead. ·

Starbuck passed a hand over the man's eyes. Then he rose to his feet and stood staring down at the body. He heard again those last words and any lingering doubt was dispelled. Proof positive lay dead at his feet. The bastard had called him by name! And hammered him to the cross with one last breath.

He was indeed a fool!

Chapter Eleven

The sun was a fiery ball lodged in the sky. Across the plains, a shimmering haze like spun glass bathed the land in a glow of illusion. Far in the distance, waves of heat pulsed and vibrated, distilling small mirages under glaring shafts of light. A faraway knoll sometimes seemed touchable and the plains went on forever.

Starbuck was roughly a hundred fifty miles northwest of Hole-in-the-Wall. He'd followed the old Bridger Trail for three days, with the Big Horn Range to the east and the Absaroka Mountains to the west. Early that morning, north of Stinking Water River, he'd crossed the line into Montana. Now, with the sun fading westward, he intersected the Bozeman Trail. A tributary of the Yellowstone flowed through the juncture, providing fresh water and plentiful graze for the gelding. He decided to pitch camp for the night.

A stand of trees along the stream afforded shelter and a ready supply of deadwood. He unsaddled, then hobbled the bay and turned him loose on a grassy stretch near the shoreline. He dumped his gear on the ground and left the rifle propped against a tree. After collecting an armload of wood, he built a small fire. Nights were brisk, the temperature plummeting when

the sun went down and a cheery blaze was one of the
few comforts on the trail. He loaded a galvanized coffeepot and put it to boil on a couple of rocks beside
the flames. Supper would consist of hardtack and a
rabbit he'd shot late that afternoon. His treat would
be a tin of peaches he'd been hoarding.

With the campsite in order, he spread his bedroll
beneath the trees. He built himself a smoke and lit it
with a stick from the fire. He was reminded of the
joke Indians told among themselves. A white man
kindled a roaring blaze and backed off from it,
whereas a red man built a small fire and hovered near
its warmth. The thought did little to improve his humor, and nothing at all to dispel his guarded mood.
He stretched out on the bedroll and lay back with his
head pillowed on the saddle. He stared at the muslin
blue of the sky and wondered where it would all end.

The killing at Cheever's Flats was still very much
on his mind. Several things were immediately apparent. The dead man, despite his denial, was yet another
of Ira Lloyd's stooges. He'd returned to Cheever's
Flats for the express purpose of verifying whether
Starbuck had been killed at Hole-in-the-Wall. In the
event that gambit had failed, he was doubtless under
orders to pick up Starbuck's trail and arrange an ambush. The most troublesome aspect, however, was
confirmation of something Starbuck had until then
merely suspected. The dead man—along with the two
bushwhackers killed previously—had known him on
sight. Clearly, his attempts to disguise his identity
hadn't worked.

All of which added a new dimension to Ira Lloyd.
The mine owner had orchestrated a far-flung assassination plot. He had retained William Dexter, whose

role in the affair was still somewhat murky. Then he'd hired at least three veteran gunhands and set them to tracking Starbuck across the vastness of the High Plains. Obviously a stickler for detail, he had let nothing escape his attention. He had acquired Starbuck's photo—probably from one of several articles in the *Police Gazette*—and each of the hired killers had quite plainly committed it to memory. There was an overall coordination to the plot that smacked of someone with a keen mind; not unlike a wily chess player, Lloyd had made his moves with a certain analytical perception of men and events. Then, too, the magnitude of the operation indicated a large outlay of funds. No cheapskate, Lloyd was clearly willing to spend whatever it took to get the job done. He was determined and relentless, a man of craft and spidery patience. He wouldn't quit until Starbuck was dead.

A similar thought was uppermost in Starbuck's mind. He possessed his own brand of bulldog tenacity, and the word "quitter" was not part of his lexicon. Yet he was still operating somewhat in the dark. His gut feeling told him that Lloyd somehow anticipated his every move. There seemed to be a contingency plan every step along the way, and no end to the number of assassins who dogged his trail. At Cheever's Flats, he'd taken precautions to insure he wasn't followed. After searching the dead man, he had gone directly from the saloon to the trading post. There, he replenished his victuals and indulged himself with the purchase of a coffeepot. Then he rode south, toward Hole-in-the-Wall. Only after full dark had he reversed course and turned north. So he was relatively certain no one shadowed his backtrail.

What lay ahead was an altogether different story.

He planned to follow the Bozeman Trail, which par-
alleled the Yellowstone in a westerly direction. Another couple of days would put him at Fort Ellis, and
some miles past there he would swing northwest, toward the Missouri River. Four days from now, barring
the unforeseen, he would arrive in Butte. Thus far,
however, his hindsight had been considerably keener
than his foresight. The trail ahead was rough country,
desolate and virtually devoid of habitation. Ambush
sites were around every crook and turn; the terrain
was made to order for bushwhackers. For all he knew,
another of Lloyd's assassins awaited him even now.
Based on events to date, he could only surmise that
Lloyd would anticipate him once more. Whether the
next attempt would be made on the trail—or in Butte
itself—was anybody's guess. Yet he needed no crys-
tal ball for a look into the future. A pattern had been
established, and patterns were seldom broken. There
would be another attempt on his life.

The coffeepot suddenly rattled. He stubbed out
his cigarette on the ground and climbed to his feet.
With his jacknife, he cut green branches and fash-
ioned a spit. Then he dressed out the rabbit and put
it to cook over the fire. Afterward he walked to the
stream to clean his knife. He hunkered down and then
stopped, grunting softly to himself. He stared at the
blood on his hands.

And thought of Ira Lloyd.

Butte was situated directly on a mountain. The town
sprawled over and around the mountain, which was
shaped like a woman's breast and filled with the
world's richest lode of copper. Unlike other mining
camps, there was a sense of permanence to the com-

munity. Butte was the prized play-toy of millionaires.

Starbuck rode into town around midday. He left the gelding at a livery stable, and spent the next couple of hours drifting from saloon to saloon. His grubby appearance made him one of the crowd, for the miners were rough-garbed and covered with powdery grime. He casually engaged men in conversation, and kept them talking with an occasional question. He was a good listener—a master of subtle interrogation—and a few rounds of drinks bought him all the inside information. He discovered Butte was on the brink of open warfare.

The story told by the miners typified what was happening all across the West. In the 1870s, when gold was the lodestone in Butte, a man worked his claim by hand. Within a few years, however, the gold diggings petered out. At that point, large corporations bought up the claims and began exploitation of minerals locked deep within the bowels of the mountain. By the end of the decade, copper was king, and the town was controlled by bankers and financiers. Absentee owners, generally a consortium of wealthy businessmen, pulled the strings from New York and San Francisco. Their singular interest was profit—at any cost.

Technology was the key to the financiers' takeover. A new invention—dynamite—was used to blast through the rock and excavate tunnels. Underground drilling, formerly done by hand, was now accomplished with power drills, operating on compressed air. Working in tandem, dynamite and power drills made it possible to burrow far beneath the earth's surface. Some operations were thousands of feet below ground and extended for miles through a labyrinth of tunnels.

As the mines probed ever deeper into the mountainside, the danger to workers multiplied at an alarming rate. Safety measures were virtually nonexistent, and accidents became commonplace. Men were killed and maimed by cave-ins, sometimes drowned when subterranean springs flooded the tunnels, and frequently incinerated when fire swept through the timbered mine shafts. Adding fuel to the workers' discontent was a miserly pay scale of thirty cents an hour. The inevitable result was revolt and violence.

Only two years ago, the battle between management and miners had flared into open hostility at Leadville, Colorado. Workers went on strike—demanding four dollars for an eight-hour shift—and the mines closed. Owners and miners armed themselves, and Leadville teetered on the edge of anarchy. The state militia was activated and the miners were ultimately forced back to work. Yet the battle cry had been sounded all across the West.

Embittered workers rallied to the exhortations of radical union organizers. With armed men on both sides, a strike more often than not developed into a bloody confrontation. Murder, complete with bombings and midnight assassinations, was the rule. Still, the owners controlled the courts and the law, and as a last resort, the militia. Strikes were generally broken by the might of force, and the miners seldom realized any lasting benefit. The struggle, nonetheless, continued unabated. A climate of revolution spread like wildfire throughout western mining camps.

Even now a strike was brewing in Butte. Starbuck learned that labor leaders were organizing the miners along military lines. Weapons were being distributed, and rifle squads were openly training in the surrounding hills. The plan was to call a general strike, and challenge the owners with their own tactics. The hired guns of management—known as goon squads—and the militia would be met by organized resistance. The battle lines were drawn and an explosion was imminent. Butte was where the union leaders would take their stand.

Starbuck discovered the impending strike directly affected his own plans. The Grubstake Mining Company—owned by Ira Lloyd—had suspended operations. The mine had been closed almost a month past, with no prior warning of a shutdown. Several miners attributed the closing to the threat of a strike. Grubstake management apparently preferred to sit out the battle and wait until the dust settled. As for Ira Lloyd himself, the name was unknown in Butte's saloons. George Horwell, the general manager, had operated the mine for the last three years. The day after the shutdown he had simply vanished from town. No one could hazard a guess as to where he'd gone.

Late that afternoon, Starbuck went to have a look for himself. The Grubstake was located on the west side of the mountain, near the bottom of the slope. Everything he'd heard was substantiated by what he found. The windows and door of the office were boarded up, and the mine shaft was sealed off by heavy timbers. There was no watchman, and no evidence anyone had been near the place in several weeks. For all practical purposes, the mine appeared abandoned.

Unless William Dexter was a fool, he'd known the Grubstake was closed when he offered Starbuck

the assignment. Then, too, it seemed curiously strange
that Ira Lloyd was a cipher to everyone in Butte. On
top of that, there was the additional mystery of
George Horwell, the Grubstake manager. Why he'd
disappeared and where he'd gone were equal parts of
the overall riddle. The upshot of all these imponder-
ables was a cul-de-sac. A dead end that seemingly
stopped at Butte.

Starbuck took a room in one of the local hotels.
His investigation was stymied and he was momentarily at a loss. A bath and a decent meal and a good
night's sleep seemed very much in order. He would
think on it overnight and then decide his next move.

For the next move might very well be the last.

Starbuck rolled out of bed and padded barefoot to the
washstand. He poured water from a pitcher into a
cracked basin and briskly scrubbed his face. After
rinsing his mouth, he smoothed his hair back and
caught his reflection in the mirror. The vestiges of
Hole-in-the-Wall marked his features.

The bridge of his nose was slightly off center and
an angry scar still puckered one eyebrow. The puffi-
ness was gone from his lip, but a hairline crease was
visible. He looked vaguely like a pugilist who had
stepped into the prize ring once too often. He wondered how Lola would react when she got a glimpse
of the rearrangement. Then he laughed at himself for
wondering at all.

After supper last night, he'd gone on a quick
shopping spree. A men's emporium was able to outfit
him in a suit and accessories that were reasonably
passable. He had swapped the Stetson for a derby,
and chucked the range garb, including the vest and

the conchas belt, into a trash bin. His last purchase was a straight razor and a soap mug. Then he'd walked down to the livery stable and sold the bay. He got a good price, but it made the chore no easier. The horse had served him well.

Pouring fresh water, he lathered his face and shaved with dull concentration. His thoughts this morning were not on the bay, and only fleetingly on Lola Montana. He was, instead, mentally preparing himself to assume a new guise. He finished shaving and toweled his face dry. Then he dressed, remembering to remove the fake dead tooth, and walked out the door. He left nothing of Arapahoe Smith behind.

By eight o'clock, he'd had breakfast and inquired directions to the sheriff's office. A cheap cigar was wedged in the corner of his mouth, and the derby was cocked at a rakish angle. He thought it added just the right touch to his cover story. Hurrying along the street, he worked himself into the proper mood of outrage. He stormed into the sheriff's office with a look of bellicose indignation.

Hiram Urschel was less lawman than politician. He was bald and potbellied, and wore thick, wire-rimmed glasses. He was also the tool of the mine owners, and currently sitting on a powder keg called Butte. He looked nervous as a whore in church.

"Earl Suggs," Starbuck announced, shaking his hand. "Western District Manager for the Olympic Mining Equipment Company."

"Yessir," Urschel replied without much interest. "What can I do for you, Mr. Suggs?"

"I have just now," Starbuck remarked stiffly, "come from the Grubstake mine. Or perhaps I should say—what's left of the mine!"

"You have some connection with the Grubstake?"

"I do indeed!" Starbuck thundered. "To the tune of a hundred thousand dollars."

"A hundred—"

"Precisely!" Starbuck assumed a wrathful stance. "An Olympic smelter—Model ZB10—ordered by Grubstake and due to arrive here tomorrow morning!"

"Oh!" Urschel nodded sagely. "Grubstake ordered the smelter and promised payment on delivery. That the idea?"

"Scoundrels!" Starbuck stumped to the window and back again, puffing clouds of smoke. "Sheriff, I desperately need your assistance! Otherwise I am in dire jeopardy of losing my job. Where might I find the Grubstake's owner, Mr. Ira Lloyd?"

"Don't know any Lloyd," Urschel advised him. "The owner of record is a man named William Dexter. He's headquartered in Denver."

"I—" Starbuck was genuinely astounded. "How did you come by that information?"

Urschel nervously drummed his fingers on the desktop. "Guess there's no harm in telling you that. I was asked to contact all the mine owners and coordinate things when this strike blows. I wrote Dexter about six weeks ago." He paused, wiped his nose. "The only reply I got was the one you've seen for yourself. He closed down the mine."

"And you've never heard of Ira Lloyd?"

"Not till you mentioned the name."

"Have you ever met Dexter?"

"No, I haven't," Urschel admitted. "Course, that's neither here nor there. Most of the mines are owned by syndicates or fronts—"

"Fronts?"

"Dummy corporations," Urschel explained. "So it's not surprising we never see the individuals themselves."

"Sheriff, just between us . . ." Starbuck winked and munched his cigar. "Would you say Dexter is a front man?"

Urschel gave him a hard, wise look. "That'd be my educated guess."

"Do you recall when he bought the Grubstake?"

"Well, as I recollect, it was about three years ago. Sometime the spring or early summer of '79."

"Uh-huh!" Starbuck deliberated a moment. "What about the manager, George Horwell? Any idea where I might locate him?"

"Wouldn't have the least notion."

"Out of curiosity"—Starbuck made an offhand gesture with his cigar—"what does he look like . . . his general appearance?"

"Let's see," Urschel said in a mild, abstracted way. "Early thirties, brown hair, medium height, slim build; pretty average. Why do you ask?"

"No reason."

Starbuck thought the reason was best kept to himself. He now knew what had happened to the Grubstake manager. George Horwell had died on a barroom floor at Cheever's Flats. Which partially explained his disappearance from Butte, and raised yet another intriguing question.

Was Horwell otherwise known as Ira Lloyd? Or, carrying it a step further . . . *was there an Ira Lloyd?*

Chapter Twelve

Starbuck pulled into Union Station three mornings later. From Butte he had traveled to Salt Lake City, and there he'd caught the overnight train to Denver. He looked worn and hollow-eyed from the long trip, and his mood was one of quiet steel fury. He planned to brace William Dexter.

All the way from Butte he'd brooded on his next step. There were no easy answers, only hard questions. The man he'd killed at Cheever's Flats was undoubtedly George Horwell, the Grubstake manager. Whether or not Horwell and Ira Lloyd were one and the same was less certain. Try as he might, he had thought of no way to establish a connection. Nor was there any practical way to determine Horwell's link to Dutch Henry Horn. As for the knottier question— did Ira Lloyd actually exist?—he was in a complete quandary. Key pieces to a very convoluted puzzle were still missing.

Yet certain factors were beyond question. By whatever name, someone had organized an elaborate assassination plot. There was a direct link between that someone and a ghost from his past, Dutch Henry Horn. Which meant there had been a concerted effort to keep tabs on him over the last seven years. His reputation as a detective was known, and someone had skillfully employed it as a device to lure him into a trap. Further, though the reason was unclear, there was obviously some reluctance to assassinate him in Denver. Otherwise there was no need to rig such a complex scheme, one that enticed him out of the city. He could easily have been killed on homeground.

So all roads led back to Denver. The case had begun with William Dexter, and he was clearly the key to the missing pieces. There was, moreover, the very real possibility that he alone had orchestrated the assassination plot. If true, that would explain his ownership of the Grubstake mine and unravel, at last, the mystery of Ira Lloyd. For if William Dexter had invented Ira Lloyd, the case was closed. With the exception of one final question.

What was his link to Dutch Henry Horn?

Starbuck was determined to have an answer. He'd been shot at and beaten to a pulp, and conned so thoroughly he felt like the greenest of rubes. He was in no mood for polite conversation or civilized tactics. His plan was simple and direct, versed in terms even a hotshot Denver lawyer would understand. He intended to put a gun to Dexter's head.

From the train depot, Starbuck took a hansom cab uptown. He got off at the corner of Eighteenth and Larimer, and walked directly to the Barclay Building. An elevator deposited him on the fifth floor, and he proceeded along the hallway to a suite of offices. Entering the waiting room, he found a male secretary seated behind a desk. The man was slightly built, somewhat bookish in appearance. He glanced up from a stack of paperwork, nodded pleasantly.

"Good morning."

Starbuck halted before the desk. "Tell Dexter I

want to see him. The name's Luke Starbuck."

The man's smile faltered. "Apparently you haven't heard, Mr. Starbuck."

"Heard what?"

"About Mr. Dexter," the man stammered. "He—he's dead."

"Dead!" Starbuck stopped, as though he'd walked into a wall. His mouth hardened, and when he spoke the words were clipped, brittle. "How'd it happen?"

"He was shot . . . murdered."

"By who?"

"No one knows." The man swallowed, eyes grim. "He worked late one night, and the next morning—it was awful—I found him myself."

Starbuck's tone was inquisitorial. "Any signs of a struggle?"

"No, sir."

"Was he robbed?"

"Oh, no!" the man blurted. "There was considerable cash in his wallet and he was wearing a very valuable timepiece. His person was . . . undisturbed."

"Anything missing from the office files—records or correspondence?"

"Nothing insofar as we've been able to determine. The police were here and went through everything very thoroughly. His safe was open—that's where he kept confidential records—and they even inspected that. Everything appeared in order."

"When was he killed?"

"Yesterday," the man said miserably. "Or to be more precise, night before last. I found him yesterday morning."

Starbuck's expression was wooden. Yet any

doubt was blown from his mind like jackstraws in a wind. *Ira Lloyd did exist!*

The timing told the tale. The lawyer had been murdered one day before Starbuck returned to Denver. As for a motive, it was patently clear he'd been silenced. Forced to talk, he could have revealed the whereabouts of Ira Lloyd. Or more important—since the name was probably phony—the true identity of Ira Lloyd. The sequence of events was not difficult to piece together.

Some ten days ago, Starbuck had killed Horwell. Then he'd appeared in Butte and begun asking questions. Somehow word had reached Lloyd, and he had correctly anticipated Starbuck's next move. With Butte a washout, Starbuck would return to Denver and put the screws on Dexter. Having failed to kill Starbuck—and unwilling to risk exposure—Lloyd had taken the only remaining countermove. He'd killed Dexter.

Starbuck pondered it at length. His eyes narrowed in concentration and he mentally shifted the pieces on the chess board once more. Then he nodded to himself, satisfied with the result. Finally, his gaze shifted to the man behind the desk.

"What's your name?"

"Frank Huggins."

"Do you know me, Mr. Huggins?"

"Yessir," Huggins murmured. "That is to say, I know who are you are, Mr. Starbuck."

"Suppose I took you into my confidence?" Starbuck arched one eyebrow in question. "Would I be safe in assuming you'd keep it to yourself?"

"Oh, yessir!" Huggins said with a catch in his voice. "I would never betray a confidence!"

"I'd want your word," Starbuck warned him. "And I can't abide a man who breaks his word."

Huggins bobbed his head. "You have my solemn oath, Mr. Starbuck."

"Good enough." Starbuck paused, let him hang a moment. "I was working on a case for Mr. Dexter. Unless I'm wrong, the subject of that investigation is the man who killed him."

"You really mean it?"

"I'd bet on it," Starbuck said with conviction. "But I'll need your help to prove it."

"Anything!" Huggins offered. "Anything at all!"

"I need a look at Mr. Dexter's confidential files— the ones in the safe."

"Oh, my!" Huggins said doubtfully. "The police wouldn't like that, Mr. Starbuck. Chief Kelsey himself ordered me not to touch anything until they've finished their investigation."

"Who's to know?" Starbuck smiled. "I won't tell him if you don't."

"Well—"

"You want to help catch the killer, don't you?"

"Yes, of course!"

"Then here's your chance," Starbuck urged. "I'll be in and out before you know it."

"I . . ." Huggins hesitated, then suddenly squared himself up. "I'll do it! I owe that much to Mr. Dexter."

"That's the ticket!"

Starbuck quickly crossed the room. He entered Dexter's private office and stopped just inside the door. The office was richly appointed, with a carved walnut desk, several wingback chairs, and plush carpeting. Someone had carefully washed the desktop, but the outline of bloodstains was still visible. A cursory inspection indicated the lawyer had been shot while seated in the judge's chair behind the desk. From the pattern of the bloodstains, he had then slumped forward on the desk, apparently shot in the head. All signs pointed to a swift and efficient job. An execution, and not the work of a stranger.

After a look around, Starbuck began with the desk. He spent the next half hour rummaging through Dexter's personal effects. He was searching for anything that might provide a lead to either Ira Lloyd or the Grubstake Mining Company. Curiously, there was no correspondence from George Horwell, the mine manager. Odder still, there was no file pertaining to the mine itself. It was as though all traces of the Grubstake had been expunged from Dexter's records.

The squat wall safe was a trove of information. The contents revealed that Dexter's business interests had been varied and immensely profitable. A large bookkeeping ledger was particularly enlightening. There, page by page, was a detailed record of the lawyer's financial dealings. His association with men of power and wealth ranged from Denver to San Francisco, with notable emphasis on mining investments. The pages were in chronological order, providing a calendar with dates and company names and dollar figures. Between April, 1879, and May, 1879, Starbuck made a startling discovery. A page had been neatly razored from the ledger.

The missing page was proof in itself. He recalled an item gleaned from his conversation with the sheriff in Butte. Three years ago—which translated to the spring of 1879—William Dexter had purchased the Grubstake mine. The time frame fit perfectly, and

the missing page, by its very absence, was strong testimony. All transactions relating to the Grubstake had
been removed from the ledger. Which meant Dexter
was, in the end, a mere front man.

The motive behind the killing was now corroborated. No record existed connecting Dexter to Ira
Lloyd. Nor was there any fear of the lawyer's talking.

A dead man was indeed a silent partner.

Starbuck paused at the corner of Fourteenth and Larimer. He lit a cigarette and stood looking at the police
station. He was thinking without any charity of Chief
Elwood Kelsey. Their dislike was mutual and of long
duration. Yet he saw no alternative to requesting the
chief's cooperation. He desperately needed a lead.

A dull and grinding weariness had fallen over
him on his walk from the Barclay Building. Any trace
of Ira Lloyd had ended at the lawyer's office. There
was no next step, for the missing page from the ledger
had effectively erased the trail. His investigation was
blunted, and with nowhere left to turn, his only option
was the police. He would attempt, however briefly, to
resurrect William Dexter. A voice from the grave
might yet be made to speak.

Inside the police station, Starbuck was left to cool
his heels for nearly an hour. He understood the slight
was intentional, a low form of insult meant to em-
barrass him. Denver's chief of police was contemptuous of private detectives in general, and he reserved
a particularly virulent animosity for Starbuck. Based
in part on envy, his attitude blackened in direct pro-
portion to Starbuck's reputation. A quote in a newspaper interview had revealed the sum and substance

of his spite. He had publicly labeled the manhunter a licensed killer.

Smoking quietly, Starbuck waited on a bench in the hall. He'd learned long ago that the man who lost his temper generally lost the fight. The winner, inevitably, was the man who provoked his opponent into some heedless act. He took a tight grip on himself, and ruthlessly suppressed his anger. He couldn't afford to lose today.

At length, a uniformed officer ushered him into the chief's office. Elwood Kelsey was a beefy man, with the bulbous nose of a heavy drinker and the girth of one who indulged himself in the good life. His eyes were small and mean, and he looked marvelously like a bright pig. He let Starbuck stand, hat in hand.

"You wanted to see me?"

"I'm working on a case." Starbuck regarded him with great calmness. "I'd like your assistance."

"God's blood!" Kelsey declared hotly. "Aren't you the bold one! Do you really believe I'd give you the time of day?"

"You will when you hear my client's name."

"And who might that be?"

"William Dexter."

Kelsey was visibly startled. "Why would Dexter hire a—someone like you?"

"He retained me to find a man," Starbuck lied easily. "I have reason to believe that same man killed him."

"What's the man's name?"

Starbuck was alert to any reaction. "Ira Lloyd."

"Never heard of him." Kelsey's eyebrows drew together in a frown. "Who is he?"

"A stock promoter," Starbuck said guilelessly.

"Works out of Butte . . . mostly mining stocks."

"What was his business with Dexter?"

"Let's trade." Starbuck met his gaze with an amused look. "You tell me your secrets and I'll tell you mine."

"Why should I help the likes of you?"

"You've got no choice," Starbuck bluffed. "I know something you don't . . . and it might solve the case."

"Bastard!" Kelsey's lips were tight and bloodless. "Go ahead, then! Ask your questions and be damned!"

"What physical evidence did you turn up at Dexter's office?"

"None," Kelsey answered with defensive gruffness. "Whoever murdered him left the place clean as a hound's tooth."

"How about the coroner's report?"

"One shot," Kelsey said in a resigned voice. "Powder burns on the right temple and no exit wound."

"No exit wound," Starbuck repeated slowly. "What caliber gun?"

"A thirty-two," Kelsey replied. "All the same, the autopsy showed death was instantaneous."

"So he knew the killer." Starbuck was thoughtful a moment, then went on. "Any eyewitnesses? Someone who saw the man entering or leaving the building?"

"Not so far."

"Was the door to Dexter's office forced?"

"No." Kelsey's tone was emphatic. "Either it wasn't locked, or he admitted the killer without incident."

"Anything else?" Starbuck insisted. "Anything unusual or out of place . . . maybe something you confiscated as evidence?"

"Nothing." Kelsey halted, glaring at him. "Now it's your turn! What was Dexter's interest in this fellow Lloyd?"

Starbuck embroidered on his original fairy tale. "Lloyd swindled one of his clients. Don't ask which one, because Dexter never told me."

"Where's Lloyd now?"

"I lost his trail in Butte."

"Butte?" Kelsey gave him a dirty look. "Are you saying you can't place Lloyd in Denver at the time of the murder?"

"I can't place him at all." Starbuck stitched a smile across his face. "I've never laid eyes on the man."

"You tricked me!"

"No, Chief," Starbuck said without irony. "You tricked yourself."

"I'll get you!" Kelsey's fist crashed into the desktop. "By the sweet Jesus, I'll run you out of Denver!"

Starbuck stared him straight in the eye, challenging him. "You haven't got the balls for it—or the clout."

Kelsey reddened with apoplectic rage. Starbuck flipped him a salute and walked to the door. Outside, however, the smile slipped and he admitted to himself it was a hollow victory. While he had won the game of wits, nothing of any value had been uncovered. He'd hopscotched his way back to square one.

Late that afternoon Starbuck entered the First National Bank. An hour earlier he had called a political marker with Lou Blomger, the underworld czar of Denver. In his pocket was a court order, duly executed by a circuit judge. He thought it a shot in the dark, but nonetheless worth a try. He'd exhausted his options.

Andrew Reed, the bank president, was portly and urbane, with foxy eyes and bone-china teeth. He was a high priest of Denver society, and a man of such vanity that he knelt only before mirrors. He looked up as Starbuck pushed through the swinging door of the balustrade and approached his desk. His greeting was civil but cool.

"Good afternoon, Mr. Starbuck."

"Afternoon." Starbuck handed him the court order. "As you'll see, that authorizes me to inspect the bank records of William Dexter."

"Highly irregular!" Reed squinted owlishly, rapidly scanning the paper. "May I inquire your purpose?"

"Confidential," Starbuck said vaguely. "But just between us, there's some hitch in getting Dexter's will probated."

"Indeed?" Reed spread his hands in a bland gesture. "I presume you are representing the widow?"

Starbuck shrugged off the question. "Hope there won't be any problem having a look at the records."

"Perish the thought!" Reed smiled dutifully. "The First National always honors a lawful request."

"Judge Peters told me you were a man of high principle."

"We all serve the public, Mr. Starbuck. Indeed we do!"

Reed summoned the head teller and issued instructions. Starbuck was then led along a corridor and

into a back room filled with filing cabinets. He asked
to see William Dexter's records for the last three
years. A clerk went through the files, and returned
with three enormous ledgers. Seated at a table, Starbuck began with the ledger marked 1879. He soon
struck paydirt.

Beginning the summer of 1879, a draft from the
Grubstake Mining Company had been deposited to
William Dexter's business account on the first of each
month. Leafing through the ledgers, Starbuck discovered the practice had continued month by month,
without interruption. The amounts were sizable and
grew progressively larger, indicating the mine had
prospered. Then, only a month ago, the deposits had
abruptly ceased. The date coincided with the closing
of the mine.

There were hundreds of entries in the ledgers,
covering Dexter's transactions in myriad business
ventures. The sheer volume of it left Starbuck bleary-
eyed, and his concentration on the mine almost cost
him a vital clue. Then, so suddenly it took his breath
away, he tumbled to a pattern. On the first of each
month the Grubstake Mining draft had been credited
to the account. On the fifth of each month a draft had
been drawn and debited against the account. The
practice had been regularly followed, month after
month, and the tipoff was a simple matter of calculation. The debits—to the penny—were ten percent
less than the amount of the Grubstake deposits.

The conclusion was inescapable. William Dexter,
functioning as a front man, had taken ten percent off
the top for overseeing the Grubstake operation. Those
monthly drafts for the balance were clearly earmarked
for the lawyer's silent partner. The entries in the ledg-

ers showed the drafts were always made to the order of the same firm, in the same location. The Black Hills Land Company. Deadwood, Dakota Territory.

Starbuck knew where to look for Ira Lloyd.

Chapter Thirteen

They were naked. The night was warm and modesty unnecessary. Stretched out on the bed, a tangle of arms and legs, their breath grew shorter. He kissed the nape of her neck, and they silently caressed and fondled. He cupped one of her breasts and the nipple swelled erect. She moaned, exhaled a hoarse, whimpering cry. Then his hand slowly slid down her stomach and went lower still until she shuddered convulsively.

"Oh Luke," she gasped in his ear. "Oooo—"

A knock sounded at the door. Starbuck raised himself up on one elbow, his head turned toward the sitting room. She pulled him back down in a fierce embrace. Her voice was furry and passionate.

"Forget it!" she whispered urgently. "They'll go away!"

The knock turned to a hammered pounding. Starbuck kissed the tip of her nose and gently disengaged himself from her arms. He rolled out of bed and moved to the wardrobe.

"Jeezus Christ!" Lola cursed furiously. "What a sense of timing!"

"Won't take long," Starbuck grumbled. "I'll send the bastard packing!"

"Watch yourself, lover!" Lola cautioned, suddenly wary. "One beating gives a man's face character. No need to overdo a good thing!"

"You've got my vote on that."

Starbuck hastily slipped into shirt and pants. He took the Colt from beneath his pillow and walked to the bedroom door. The pounding grew louder as he padded barefoot across the sitting room. He hurried the last few steps through the foyer.

"Hold your horses!" he yelled. "I hear you!"

The Colt at waist level, he cautiously flattened himself against the wall. Then he cracked open the door and took a quick peek. A look of astounded disbelief swept his features.

"Butch!"

"Howdy, Arapahoe!" Butch grinned. "Bet you wasn't expectin' me."

"I sure as the devil wasn't!" Starbuck opened the door wider. "How the hell'd you find me, anyway?"

"Asked around." Butch sauntered into the foyer. "Finally got a line on you from a barkeep in some dive."

"Where'd you come from?"

"Cheyenne," Butch replied absently. "I left my horse there and caught a train. Got in a couple of hours ago."

"Well—" Starbuck closed the door, still bemused. "C'mon in and tell me about it. What's up?"

Butch stopped just inside the entranceway. He stood for a moment eyeballing the sitting room, and his grin dissolved into a look of wonder. He tilted his hat back on his head, whistled softly.

"Holy cow!" he muttered. "You got yourself some digs!"

"Nothing much." Starbuck motioned him to a

chair. "Take a load off your feet and give me the lowdown."

"Don't mind if I do." Butch dropped into an easy chair, and suddenly noticed his bare feet. "Sorry I woke you up, Luke. What I got to say wouldn't keep till morning."

Starbuck flicked a glance toward the bedroom door, then shrugged. He saw the bulge of a sixgun beneath the youngster's jacket, carried on the off side and jammed into the waistband. The pistol was no surprise, but the kid materializing out of the night was like a dash of ice water. He laid his Colt on the coffee table and took a seat on the sofa.

"What's so important you'd risk coming to Denver?"

"Aww, I'm safe enough," Butch said confidently. "No dodgers out on a little fish like me. Course, the same don't hold true for Mike! That's why he asked me to come in his place."

"Mike sent you?" Starbuck asked, confounded. "All the way from Hole-in-the-Wall?"

"Well, don't you see, he wasn't sure whether you'd settled matters up in Butte. How'd things work out?"

"I was a day late and a dollar short. No sign of our friend."

"Then my trip wasn't wasted! Mike figured we'd be better off safe than sorry."

"You still haven't told me why?"

"Got a message for you," Butch replied. "Mike says—"

Lola appeared in the bedroom door. Her hair hung loose and she was wrapped in a filmy peignoir. The sheer fabric accentuated her full breasts and the

curve of her hips. She glided into the room and struck
a provocative pose beside the sofa.

"Who's your friend, lover?"

Starbuck was amused by her dramatic entrance,
and her choice of costume. His arm moved in an idle
gesture. "Lola Montana, meet Butch Cassidy."

"Hello, Butch," Lola purred. "Any friend of
Luke's is a friend of mine."

Butch swept off his hat and bounded to his feet.
His mouth sagged open and he ogled her with a look
of slack-jawed amazement. He seemed to have lost
his voice.

"What's the matter, honey?" Lola flashed a theatrical smile. "Cat got your tongue?"

"No, ma'am!" Butch sputtered. "Pleased to make
your acquaintance."

"Ma'am?" Lola uttered a low, throaty laugh.
"God, I must be losing my touch!"

"No, ma'am!" Butch twisted his hat into knots. "I
mean—no offense, ma'am—you ain't lost nothin'!"

"That's sweet! I think I'm going to like you,
Butch."

Lola fluttered her lashes and sized him up with a
quick once-over. Her immediate impression was of a
young ruffian fresh off a cattle drive. He smelled of
horses and leather, and distant familiarity with a bath-
tub. Yet, beneath the dithering and callow manner,
there was the sense of a kid aged beyond his years.
She wondered what business he had with a manhunter.

"Lookee here now, Luke!" Butch blushed beet
red, took a step toward the door. "I'm sorry as all

get-out! Wouldn't've busted in here if I knowed you had . . . company."

"Simmer down," Starbuck said genially. "You're not interrupting anything that won't keep."

"Why, of course not!" Lola trilled. "We were just sitting around chewing the fat!"

Starbuck caught the mockery in her eyes, and chuckled softly. "Lola's a good sport, Butch. She knows it's business before pleasure with me."

"You're sure?" Butch glanced from one to the other. "I ain't all that wet behind the ears. You just say the word and I'll get lost!"

"Stick around," Lola said with a sigh of resignation. "I'll just make myself scarce and let you boys get on with your talk. I don't mind."

Starbuck made a spur-of-the-moment decision. In all the time he'd known her, Lola had never once pried into his business affairs. She respected his privacy with grace and with no hint of resentment. Yet, at times, he sensed she was hurt by his cynical distrust, which until now had included her. The thought suddenly occurred that she deserved better. He decided to give it a try.

"You stick around, too." He patted the sofa. "Have a seat, and let's hear what Butch has to say. He's come a long way to say it."

Lola felt her heart skip a beat. She realized their relationship—at that very instant—had undergone a change. Tonight, for the first time, he was extending his trust. She knew she'd passed a critical test, and sensed they were now something more than lovers. She promised herself he would never regret the decision.

When she was seated, Starbuck turned his attention to Butch. "You said you've got a message?"

"Yeah, I do." Butch resumed his chair. "Mike wasn't sure whether it meant anything, but he sent me along all the same. He figured you ought to judge for yourself."

"Go on."

"Well, he got to doing some powerful thinking after you left Hole-in-the-Wall. He wouldn't admit it, but the two of you being set up by this Ira Lloyd must've thrown him for a loop. Anyway, he remembered something he'd all but forgot."

"About Dutch Henry Horn?"

"For a fact," Butch said, suddenly solemn. "Dutch Henry was a widower."

"I'll be damned!" Starbuck was momentarily nonplussed. "I never heard anything about Dutch Henry being married."

"Nobody else, either," Butch noted. "Mike said she was some sort of big, dark secret. When him and Dutch Henry rode together, none of the rest of the gang knowed about her. Only reason he told Mike was because they were partners."

"Where did she live?"

"Outside Fort Worth a ways. Dutch Henry had a farm he used for a cover."

"Did Mike ever meet her?"

"Nope." Butch shook his head. "He never had no reason to go there, and he wasn't invited."

"When was she supposed to have died?"

"Near as Mike recollects, it was about a year before him and Dutch Henry parted company. So that would've made it sometime late summer of '74."

"If Mike never saw her or the farm"—Starbuck

fixed him with a stern look—"then how come he's so sure she actually died?"

"He asked himself the same question," Butch admitted. "There for a while he even toyed with the notion that Ira Lloyd might turn out to be Horn's wife. If she hadn't died, it could've been her tryin' to kill you both with one stone."

"What changed his mind?"

"Like I said," Butch reminded him, "Mike give it a lot of thought. He remembered Dutch Henry was busted up something terrible when it happened. So, all things considered, he figures it was on the up and up."

"But he still doesn't know—not for certain."

"No," Butch conceded. "Not for certain."

Starbuck nodded and was silent, thoughtful. When he looked up, there was a strange expression in his eyes. "Something else occurs to me."

"What's that?"

"As I recall, Dutch Henry was in his late thirties when I killed him."

Lola started with an involuntary gasp. It was the first and only time he'd ever referred to the darker side of his work. Starbuck and Butch glanced at her, and she smiled sheepishly. Then Butch picked up the thread of the conversation.

"I got an idea you're onto the same thing Mike was thinkin'."

"It makes sense," Starbuck said quite seriously. "A man that old—and married—it's just natural he'd have some kids. Add seven years and they'd be grown by now."

"Grown and chock-full of hate for the man that killed their daddy."

"Don't forget Mike," Starbuck amended. "He winged Dutch Henry in a shootout. That would explain why somebody put us at each other's throats."

"Them was Mike's words exactly."

"I'd say it's the best bet yet."

"Only one trouble," Butch said glumly. "We don't know where to lay our hands on Ira Lloyd. We don't even know if he's a him or a her!"

"Things turned around today," Starbuck informed him. "I got my first solid lead since this whole mess started. It's a pip, too!"

Butch's eyes lit up like soapy agates. "You know who Lloyd is?"

"No, not just exactly," Starbuck remarked. "But I've got a damn good idea where to find him."

"Where?"

"Deadwood."

"Dakota Territory?"

"Let me catch you up on what's happened."

Starbuck briefly recounted everything that had occurred since he'd departed Hole-in-the-Wall. He told of the shooting at Cheever's Flats, and how he'd eventually identified the dead man as George Horwell. Then he detailed his investigation of the Grubstake mine and his conversation with the sheriff in Butte. All of which, he noted wryly, had led him step by step into a dead end. From there, he outlined the return to Denver and the salient factors in William Dexter's murder. He went on to relate what he'd learned from Dexter's secretary and Chief Kelsey. Finally, he explained the discovery he'd made while sifting through the bank records. Though it was a paper trail, the ledgers had left him convinced on one point. Ira Lloyd was somehow connected with the Black Hills Land Company.

"So Deadwood's the place to look," he concluded. "Our man's headquartered there—whatever name he goes by."

"I dunno," Butch said skeptically. "Them ledgers don't exactly *prove* it's Lloyd. Sounds like Dexter had so many irons in the fire it'd be hard to tell one way or the other."

"There's more to it than that." Starbuck paused, and the timbre of his voice changed. "Late yesterday I went back and had another talk with Dexter's secretary. He let slip a real curious item."

"What d'you mean?"

"Dexter only left Denver twice a year on business."

"Where'd he go?"

"That's the curious part." Starbuck pondered a moment, and then, almost as though he were thinking out loud, he went on. "Dexter never told anyone where he was headed. According to his secretary, it was all hush-hush and top-drawer secret."

"So you drew another blank?"

"No," Starbuck elaborated. "I went to the train station and questioned the ticket agents. Things got curiouser and curiouser once I jiggled their memory."

"You did it!" Butch whooped wildly. "You found out where Dexter went on those trips!"

"Yankton." Starbuck's pale eyes glittered, and a wide grin spread across his face. "Dakota Territory."

"Yankton?" Butch appeared bewildered. "I thought you said Lloyd's headquarters was in Deadwood."

"Yankton's the territorial capital. The train line

from the east ends there, and Cheyenne's the closest railhead to the west. The last leg of the trip to Deadwood—whatever direction you're coming from—has to be made by stagecoach."

"Are you saying Dexter went on by stage to Deadwood?"

"Maybe," Starbuck mused. "On the other hand, Deadwood's a little rough for a city slicker like Dexter. I'm willing to bet him and Lloyd got their heads together in Yankton. It figures he'd deliver a report on the Grubstake operation at least twice a year."

"Why, sure!" Butch said, suddenly grasping it. "If he was headed for Deadwood, why go the long way around through Yankton?"

"Exactly," Starbuck affirmed. "The shorter way would've been Cheyenne, and on from there by stage. He'd have saved a couple of days in both directions."

"By golly, that pretty well nails it down!"

"One other thing." Starbuck's expression turned sober, somehow pensive. "Dexter was killed with a thirty-two. That's a gentleman's gun and I've got a strong suspicion Lloyd did the job himself."

"You mean he was here in Denver?"

"I doubt he would've trusted the job to a hired hand. Not to mention the files on the Grubstake and the missing page out of Dexter's ledger. He had to get it right the first time—no mistakes."

"Well, a thirty-two might be a gentleman's gun, but he sure don't act like one. Not the way he kills people."

Starbuck's jawline tightened. "His killing days are about to stop."

Butch gave him a quick, intent look. "You're headed for Deadwood, aren't you?"

"I was." Starbuck pulled at his ear, reflective. "Figured to leave tomorrow morning. But I think I just changed my mind."

"Why so?"

"A day more or less won't matter. We might do well to check out a few headstones—down in Pueblo."

"What's in Pueblo?"

"That's where I killed Dutch Henry."

The shadow of a question clouded Butch's eyes. "Am I going deaf, or did you say 'we'?"

"Why not?" Starbuck commented. "That way there's no loose ends. You'll be able to give Mike the whole story."

"Suits me," Butch said with an impish grin. "I don't get much chance to work the right side of the law."

"Tell you what." Starbuck hesitated, considering. "Go downstairs and see the desk clerk. Have him fix you up with a room, and tell him I said to put it on my bill."

"Say, thanks a lot, Luke!"

"I'll roust you out about sunup."

"Sunup!" Butch rolled his eyes. "Why so early?"

"The train for Pueblo leaves at seven."

"You know, I got an idea rustlin' cows beats the whey outta this detective business."

Starbuck laughed and showed him to the door. Walking back to the sitting room, he stopped and stood for a moment, lost in concentration. Lola bounced off the sofa and moved to join him. Her eyes suddenly shone and she mimicked his dour expression. She slipped inside his arms.

"No more detective business tonight!"

"Yeah?"

"Yeah!" she said with a bawdy wink. "We've got some business ourselves. Unfinished business!"

"Well—" Starbuck playfully swatted her rump. "Never leave a job half done. That's my motto!"

Lola purred and led him toward the bedroom. Her look was one of smoky sensuality, and she shed the peignoir as they went through the door. Her bare white bottom blink-blinked like a beacon in the night.

Starbuck went willingly.

Chapter Fourteen

is gaze was drawn to the outhouse. The door was shut and the latch bar firmly in place. But the latch-string stopped swaying even as he watched. Someone was in the outhouse.

Starbuck suddenly whirled, leveling the Colt, and drilled a hole through the outhouse door. Thumbing the hammer back, he drew a steady bead on the door, then called out in a hard voice.

"Dutch Henry, you got a choice. Come out with your hands up, or I'll turn that privy into a sieve."

"Hold off, Starbuck! I'm comin' out, you win!"

The latch bar lifted and the door cracked open. Horn stood in a spill of sunlight, his arms raised above the doorsill. He blinked, watching Starbuck with a sardonic expression.

"You're a regular bulldog once you get started, aren't you?"

"Toss your gun out of there, Dutch! Slow and easy, nothin' fancy."

"I laid it on the seat before I opened the door."

"Then lower your hands—one at a time!—and you'd better come up empty."

"Hell, I know when I'm licked." Horn lowered his left hand, palm upraised. "See, no tricks and no—"

His right arm dropped in a flash of metal. Star-buck triggered three quick shots. The slugs stitched a neat row straight up Horn's shirtfront, bright red dots from belly to brisket. Knocked off his feet by the im-pact, Horn crashed into the back wall of the privy, then sat down on the one-holer. A pistol fell from his hand, and his head tilted at an angle across one shoulder. His eyes were opaque and lusterless, star-ing at nothing.

Starbuck walked forward and halted at the door. He lowered the hammer on his Colt, gazing down on the dead man. A smile tugged at the corner of his mouth, and he slowly shook his head.

"You should've known better, Dutch. You sure should've."

The memory echoed distantly, as though carried to him through the corridors of time. He stared out the window, watching as the train pulled into Pueblo. He saw the town had changed little in seven years, and wondered if anyone still remembered Dutch Henry Horn.

Or the young range detective who had killed him.

The train ground to a halt outside the depot. Star-buck and Butch were the first passengers off the lead coach. They stepped onto the platform and hurried toward the end of the stationhouse. The night train for Denver departed at six, and Starbuck planned to be aboard. He thought an afternoon would suffice for what he had in mind.

Walking uptown, Starbuck experienced a strong sense of *déjà vu*. The sleepy main street was much as he recalled it, and Pueblo itself had grown hardly at all in the intervening years. The hotel still occupied one corner of the main intersection, and catty-corner across from it was the bank. The afternoon was blistering hot, and it required no effort of will to transport himself backward in time. He saw it all as though it had happened yesterday.

The summer of 1876 he had tracked Dutch Henry Horn to Pueblo. There the trail vanished, but he had reason to believe Horn was hiding out in the surrounding countryside. He took a room at the hotel, confident the outlaw would show up in town. His wait lasted nearly a month; his days were spent on the hotel veranda, where he kept a lookout on the intersection. Finally, when he'd all but lost hope, his patience paid off. Dutch Henry, accompanied by two men, rode past the hotel. Suspecting nothing, they dismounted outside the bank.

Starbuck hurried to a nearby hardware store and bought a shotgun. Then, as the men exited the bank, he challenged them in the street. He killed Horn's companions in the ensuing shootout, but the outlaw ducked around the corner and fled on foot. The chase ended across town, behind an adobe cantina. There he cornered Horn in an outhouse, and killed his third man in less than ten minutes. He was duly arrested, and only then did he discover that Horn was known locally as Frank Miller. Operating under an alias, the outlaw had purchased a ranch outside town and established himself as a cattleman. He was widely respected, and the citizens of Pueblo cared little that his true occupation was as the ringleader of a gang of horse thieves. Starbuck had escaped town one jump ahead of a lynch mob.

Today, walking along the street, Starbuck recalled the incident as the turning point in his life. The assignment had been his first job as a range detective. From there, with his reputation made, he'd gone on to other cases and wider renown. That long-ago afternoon had truly been a milestone, and he saw it now with a note of irony. The death of Dutch Henry Horn had put him in the detective business to stay.

In a sense, he owed Dutch Henry a debt of gratitude. Or perhaps it was owed to Dutch Henry's ghost, and the time of reckoning had at last come around. Someone seemed determined to collect on the debt, and collect in kind. An eye for an eye and a pound of flesh, the account settled in blood. Vengeance was the purest of all motives, and by far the most sinister. Starbuck had known men to wait longer than seven years, and their revenge was no less sweet for the wait. He wondered again what Ira Lloyd was to Dutch Henry Horn.

At the courthouse, Starbuck went directly to the county clerk's office. His request to inspect certain backdated records was met with studied reluctance. The clerk finally acceded, and with Butch in tow, he was led to a storage room. The shelves were stacked with musty ledgers dating back to Civil War times. Left alone, he and Butch dug around until they located the tax rolls for 1876. Under the name Frank Miller, they found no indication of family or survivors. Their next try was the probate files, and all their suspicions were at last confirmed. Frank Miller had an heir—a son.

The records established that one James Miller had inherited the entire estate. As the sole heir, his legacy consisted of the Diamond X Ranch and several thousand head of cattle, certain parcels of town real estate, and some $40,000 on deposit at the bank. For tax purposes, the estate had been assessed at $212,000 and so entered on the county rolls.

A further search of probate-court records provided corroboration of James Miller's parentage. In his last will and testament, Dutch Henry Horn had used the alias Frank Miller. Following his death, and the subsequent publicity, his true identity had become public knowledge. The court ruled that the father's sins in no way jeopardized the son's right of inheritance. Dutch Henry Horn's estate was legally unencumbered, and judged to be wholly apart from his criminal activities. James Miller, twenty-one at the time, was awarded uncontested title to all lands and property.

His true name, duly noted in the court record, was James T. Horn.

Starbuck's immediate concern centered on James Horn's present whereabouts. It was entirely possible he still owned the Diamond X Ranch. In that event, he might be easier located than originally thought. Still, whether in Deadwood or Pueblo, one thing was abundantly clear.

Ira Lloyd was James Miller, otherwise known as James Horn.

After weighing the situation, Starbuck decided to play it close to the vest. He needed information about James Horn; assuming the man was to be found at the ranch, there was every likelihood it would bloodshed. Yet he had no wish to risk another lynch mob in Pueblo. Wary of alerting the county clerk, who looked to be a gadfly, he made no further inquiry. He determined, instead, to try another tack.

Outside the clerk's office, Starbuck huddled briefly with Butch. He intended to pay a call on the

sheriff, and he thought the conversation would best
be conducted in privacy. There was, moreover, some
slim chance the youngster might be recognized, and
he saw no reason to tempt fate. He sent Butch to wait
for him on the courthouse steps. Then he walked
down the hall to a door marked SHERIFF, PUEBLO
COUNTY. He entered without knocking.

The man seated at the desk was lean and muscular, with weather-beaten features and a soup-
strainer mustache. His gestures were restrained, his
manner brisk and businesslike. He greeted Starbuck
in a deep baritone voice.

"Help you?"

"Hope so." Starbuck smiled affably and stuck out
his hand. "I'm Luke Starbuck."

"Ernie Tucker." The lawman's handshake was
firm and his appraisal swift. "You the detective fellow, works out of Denver?"

"You got me dead to rights, Sheriff."

"Thought so," Tucker said evenly. "I was a deputy when you caused that little rhubarb a few years
back."

Starbuck stared at him. "In that case, you'll recall
I was only doing my job."

"Never said you wasn't." Tucker smiled, waved
him to a chair. "I always figured it was good riddance
to bad rubbish. Course, some folks around here don't
agree."

"Yeah," Starbuck said, seating himself. "They're
probably the same ones who wanted to stretch my
neck."

"Say, that's right!" Tucker boomed. "Ol' Walt
Johnson saved you from a lynching bee!"

"Johnson still the town marshal?"

"No more." Tucker's smile faded. "He got turned out to pasture the year after you killed Frank Miller."

"Too bad," Starbuck said tonelessly. "He was a good lawman."

"Like I said, some folks have got long memories."

"So I've learned . . . the hard way."

Tucker ruffled his brow, watchful. "What brings you to Pueblo?"

"Frank Miller." Starbuck's expression was stoic. "Or as he was better known—Dutch Henry Horn."

"That's water under the bridge, isn't it?"

"Yeah, it was," Starbuck agreed. "Till somebody started trying to kill me."

"I don't follow you."

"There's been three attempts on my life in the last month. I have reason to believe the man behind it is Dutch Henry's son—James Horn."

"Not very likely," Tucker observed. "Nobody's seen hide nor hair of him since he sold out."

"Sold out?" Starbuck's gaze narrowed. "Are you talking about the ranch?"

"Everything," Tucker said, gesturing out the window. "Town property and the ranch, the whole ball of wax. He showed up a week or so after his daddy was buried. Quick as the deeds were transferred, he put everything on the auction block. Walked away with a potful of money—a big potful!"

"How long was he here?"

"A month, maybe a little more."

"That's fast work, considering he was barely grown."

"Well, there weren't any flies on him! No, sir, he

was smart as a whip. Got top dollar for the whole shebang!"

"Where'd he come from?"

"Back east somewhere," Tucker said, with mild wonder. "Turned out Miller—Horn—had sent him off to college. Hell, you could've knocked half the town over with a feather! Nobody even knew Horn had a son."

"What was he like?"

"Quiet, but not snooty or nothing. Course, you could tell he was educated! The minute he opened his mouth there wasn't no doubt on that score."

"Did he look anything like Dutch Henry?"

"Did he ever!" Tucker laughed. "It was downright spooky! Tall and thick through the shoulders, that same tight-lipped look around the mouth. Had his daddy's eyes too—chalk blue. Queerest eyes I ever saw on a man."

"When he left here," Starbuck inquired easily, "where'd he go?"

"Nobody knows." Tucker shrugged. "The day he sold the last piece of property, he went down to the bank and got himself a draft for the whole bundle. Then he climbed on the train and took off without a by-your-leave. Nobody knew he was gone till he'd already done it!"

"Any word of him since?"

"Not a peep," Tucker said, shaking his head. "I always figured he went back east. That's what I would've done in his place."

"Why?"

"Well—" Tucker spread his hands. "What with his daddy being a horse thief and all, that would've been the natural thing to do. A young fellow wouldn't want a thing like that hanging over his head."

"How'd he feel about the way Dutch Henry died?"

Tucker leaned back in his chair, hands steepled, tapped his forefingers together. "What you're really asking is how he felt about you killing Dutch Henry?"

"That's close to the mark."

"I never heard him say," Tucker ventured. "I'll tell you one thing, though. I don't think he harbored a grudge and I don't think he'd come looking for you. He just didn't seem like the type."

"Well, Sheriff," Starbuck said, rising to his feet, "somebody's looking for me and he's working at it full time."

Tucker eyed him with a shrewd look. "You aim to kill him, don't you?"

"I don't aim to let him kill me."

"For my money, you're barking up the wrong tree."

"I guess we'll just have to wait and see."

Starbuck nodded and walked to the door. He stepped into the hall and proceeded toward the front of the courthouse. His eyes were grim, fixed straight ahead. He thought it time to put Pueblo behind him.

He'd found his ghost.

The night was pitch dark. Cinders and sparks from the engine whistled past the coach like tiny meteors. The car lights were turned low and nearly all the passengers were asleep. A rhythmic clackety-clack of wheels on steel rails punctuated the stillness.

Starbuck was staring out the window. His expression was abstracted and faraway. He'd been sitting quietly for a long while, lost in inner deliberation.

The puzzle, fitted together piece by piece, was now almost whole. In his mind's eye, he saw a vivid mosaic of where he'd been and where he was headed. Only one small part still remained out of focus and somewhat incomplete. Yet he wasn't worried, for the answer awaited him in Deadwood and he knew who to ask. A man there was in his debt.

"Penny for your thoughts."

His preoccupation was broken by Butch's voice. He turned and found the youngster watching him with a sober gaze. He lifted his shoulders in a shrug, smiled.

"Save your penny and take a guess."

"Deadwood?"

"Yeah, that and young Mr. Horn."

"You reckon you'll be able to find him? He's a regular wizard at coverin' his tracks."

Starbuck's eyes took on a distant, prophetic look. "I'll find him."

"Wonder what he's like?"

"Why do you ask?"

"Oh, I guess I've been doing a little woolgatherin' myself. Hard to figure a man like Horn."

"How so?"

"Well, I'll tell you one thing!" Butch cocked his head in a funny smile. "If I had me a college education and all that money, I sure wouldn't be running around killin' people. Nosireebob!"

"What would you be doing instead?"

"For openers, I would've kept the Diamond X."

"Dutch Henry's ranch?" Starbuck was surprised. "Operating a cattle spread's no picnic. It's a hard life."

"You're telling me!" Butch laughed. "I was

raised up on a farm, and when I got big enough, I hired on as a cowhand. Hard work and me ain't exactly strangers!"

"Where was this?"

Butch gave him a quick, guarded glance. "Utah."

"You got folks there?"

"Maybe."

"Forget I asked," Starbuck said amiably. "I wasn't trying to poke around in your personal business."

"Well—" Butch squirmed uncomfortably in his seat. "I don't suppose it'd hurt nothin'. Anybody Mike trusts is okay in my book."

"Wouldn't go any further," Starbuck promised him. "I was just interested, that's all. A man don't meet many rustlers your age."

Butch's story was a familiar one on the frontier. His parents, Max and Ann Parker, homesteaded a quarter section in southern Utah. Devout Mormons, they sowed their fields and prayed to a benevolent God for a rich harvest. All they reaped was misfortune; three straight years of drought left the crops withered and the land parched. The Parkers lost their homestead, and turned to other work to keep food on the table. Max hired out as a teamster, hauling timber, and Ann found employment at a dairy. Times were rough and the Parkers struggled to eke out an existence.

Their eldest son, Robert LeRoy Parker, was one of six children. Only fourteen at the time, the boy went to work on a neighboring ranch to supplement the family income. He was inexperienced, somewhat impressionable, and he quickly fell in with a drifter named Mike Cassidy. Posing as a saddle tramp,

Cassidy was actually engaged in stealing cattle and trailing them to ready markets in the Colorado mining camps. To young Roy, the rustler offered a life of excitement and an escape from drudgery. The law soon tumbled to their scheme, and they took off for Robbers Roost. There, fully committed to riding the owlhoot, the youngster adopted his mentor's name. He assumed the alias Butch Cassidy.

"You already know the rest," Butch concluded with an offhand gesture. "We got run out of Utah and ended up at Hole-in-the-Wall."

Starbuck studied him a moment. "Suppose you got the chance to make a clean break? Would you take it?"

"Probably not." Butch caught his eye for an instant, looked quickly away. "Mike always says, the trouble with life, it's so goddang daily. I guess that holds for me too. The straight and narrow just don't suit my style."

"How do you know?" Starbuck asked. "You've never really given it a try."

"I tried it long enough to get burnt out on psalm singin' and an empty belly."

"Well, I'm no soul-saver," Starbuck said, grinning. "But if you ever change your mind, look me up. I might be able to steer you into something that wouldn't be so 'goddang daily'."

"I'm obliged, Luke." Butch kept his gaze averted, slightly shamefaced. "I'll likely stick to rustlin', though. The way I got it figured, it beats workin' for wages."

"Suit yourself." Starbuck let it drop there. "You want to stay over in Denver awhile?"

"Naw!" Butch said cheerfully. "Mike's like an

old hen. I'd better get on back before he comes lookin' for me."

"There's a morning train to Cheyenne."

"Guess I'll catch it," Butch said without hesitation. "That'll put me on the trail to Hole-in-the-Wall by tomorrow night."

Starbuck nodded and resumed staring out the window. He pondered the future of a likable kid turned outlaw. Sooner or later, a hangman's noose or a stiff prison sentence was in the cards. Or perhaps a quicker death, at the hands of a manhunter. The thought struck a nerve, and he silently wished the youngster Godspeed. Hole-in-the-Wall was, in the end, the only choice.

He hoped they would never meet again.

Chapter Fifteen

The stage slid to a dust-smothered halt. There were nine passengers crammed inside and six more clung to the top of the coach. The driver set the foot brake with a hard kick and looped the reins around the lever. Then he leaned over the side and let loose a raspy shout.

"All out for Deadwood!"

Starbuck was the first passenger to alight from the coach. His hair was dyed raven black and a spit-curl mustache was glued to his upper lip with spirit gum. A black eyepatch, which was held in place by a narrow headband, covered his left eye. The patch broke the line of his features and further distracted attention from his general appearance. The getup he wore was an advertisement of sorts, almost a uniform. He was attired in a black frock coat and somber vest, topped off by a low-crowned hat. A diamond stickpin gleamed from his four-in-hand tie and a larger stone sparkled on his pinky finger. He looked every inch the professional gambler.

Dusting himself off, Starbuck moved to the rear of the coach. There he waited while the luggage was unloaded from the storage boot. He took a thin black cheroot from inside his coat and snipped the end with one clean bite. Then he fished out a match and lit the cigar. Puffing smoke, he hooked his thumbs in his vest and scanned the street. All around him was a tableau of bedlam in motion.

Deadwood was surrounded by the pine-forested mountains of the Black Hills. The town proper twisted through a narrow gulch, and wooden stairways intersected terraced side streets up and down the slopes. Wagons drawn by oxen clogged the main street, and bullwhackers scorched the air with curses and the sharp pop of their whips. The boardwalks were thronged with men, and the riotous atmosphere of a gold camp pervaded the town. There was a sense of carnival madness to the milling crowds and the deafening hubbub.

Some six years past, the gold rush had transformed a wooded gulch into a boomtown. Yet, like most mining camps, Deadwood still wasn't much to look at. It was simply bigger and brassier, with a population of thirty thousand, and more arriving every day. The upper end of Main Street was packed with stores and rat-infested cafés, three banks and some thirty hotels, and one public bathhouse. The lower end of town—known locally as the Bad Lands—was a beehive of saloons, gaming dives, and cheap brothels. Sanitation was virtually unknown, and ditches carved out of the rocky terrain served as sewers. The stench of refuse and unwashed men was overpowering.

Starbuck hefted his valise and walked downstreet. He thought it unlikely anyone expected him in town. The link to Deadwood, established by the bank records in Denver, was his card in the hole. James Horn had no way of knowing he'd stumbled upon the connection and at last put the pieces together. Still, he had gone to extreme measures to insure he wasn't followed. After a day's layover in Denver, spent collecting the paraphernalia for his disguise, he had secretly made his way to Cheyenne. There he'd boarded a stagecoach for the three-hundred-mile run to Dakota Territory. The trip had consumed three days and two nights, with stops in several lesser mining camps in the western reaches of the Black Hills. Today, lost in the crowds, he seemed just another gambler touring the circuit. His cover name was Ace Pardee.

At the corner of Main and Lee, he spotted the Custer Hotel. Aptly named, it honored the man responsible for Deadwood's very existence. General George Armstrong Custer, in 1874, had commanded an expedition into the Black Hills. Apart from a thousand soldiers, he was accompanied by a geologist and two reporters. The discovery of gold was duly publicized in newspapers throughout the nation. Hundreds of prospectors, in direct violation of the Laramie Treaty of 1868, immediately invaded the holy ground of the Sioux. Within a year, the hundreds turned to thousands, and the Black Hills gold rush was on. By early 1877, with the army unable to stem the flood, the government legislated yet another treaty into extinction. The Sioux's sacred Paha Sapa—the Black Hills—were opened to settlement. And Deadwood roared to life.

Starbuck was an iconoclast where government was concerned. He considered bureaucrats the blight of mankind, and lumped all politicians into two categories, the corrupt and the stupid. The army was viewed with a somewhat more charitable outlook. Yet he made an exception in the case of George Armstrong Custer. Long ago, he'd tagged the flamboyant general as an exhibitionist, with delusions of grandeur.

The Black Hills expedition was symptomatic of Custer's thirst for recognition and fame. Only two years later that same thirst led to the Battle of the Little Big Horn. By all accounts, Custer had his eye on the presidency and needed a splashy victory to garner the nomination. The 7th Cavalry had been sacrificed not to quell the Sioux, but for the greater glory of the one called Yellowhair. In Starbuck's opinion, that made Custer something worse than a meddling bureaucrat or a corrupt politician. He was a fool.

On general principles, Starbuck checked into another hotel. He paid in advance and was shown to a cubbyhole on the second floor. The furnishings consisted of a swaybacked bed, one wooden chair, and a washstand. A chipped and fading johnny-pot occupied one corner of the room. He dumped his valise on the bed and stripped to the waist. Then, gingerly avoiding his dyed hair, he took a quick bird bath. After a shave, he toweled dry and slipped into a clean shirt. Somewhat refreshed, he put on the gambler's outfit and went downstairs. The desk clerk obligingly pointed him toward the Bad Lands.

A couple of blocks down the street, Starbuck happened upon another landmark. The No. 10 Saloon, located on the edge of the Bad Lands district, was famed as Wild Bill Hickok's last watering hole. There, on a warm August day in 1876, a deadbeat named Jack McCall had shot Hickok in the back of the head. The assassin was ultimately hanged, and his victim was laid to rest in Deadwood's budding cemetery. The funeral marked the birth of a legend.

Like many westeners, Starbuck had a jaundiced view of the man a journalist had once dubbed Prince of the Pistoleers. Hickok had reputedly killed several

dozen men in gunfights, and touted himself as the
most deadly shootist on the frontier. It was commonly
believed he could drill the cork into a bottle without
touching glass, and further, that he could handle two
guns simultaneously, blazing away from the hips and
never missing the target. He was credited as well with
having brought law and order to at least two Kansas
cowtowns, Hays City and Abilene. The truth was
somewhat more mundane.

Starbuck, through friends in the law community,
had gradually put together a factual account. The
Prince of Pistoleers was a showboat and braggart,
who followed the axiom of shoot first and ask questions later. He was known to have killed six men, four
of whom had been gunned down in coldblood. The
only man he'd ever killed in the line of duty—in a
face-to-face shootout—was a drunken gambler in Abilene. Thereafter, he had toured the East as an actor,
capitalizing on his notoriety. As a peace officer, he
was a joke, and as a gunman, he was little more than
a common killer. Among those who knew him best,
he was renowned as a man who never gave the other
fellow a ghost of a chance. He always rigged the
game.

A pragmatist himself, Starbuck took few chances.
Yet he was contemptuous of any man who killed in
coldblood. Showboats like Hickok, who pandered to
the press, were almost beneath contempt. Throughout
his lifetime, Wild Bill had courted dime novelists and
eastern journalists who dealt in sensationalism. The
result was an entire mythology based on invention,
distortion, and outright lies. Hardly a noble servant of
the law, Hickok was a spinner of windy tales, all of
them about himself. The eastern reading public was

ravenous for western heroes, particularly those who were painted larger than life and possessed all the sterling attributes. Hickok simply gave them what they wanted to hear.

Walking along the street, Starbuck was struck by a curious juxtaposition in time. General George Armstrong Custer had gone under at the Little Big Horn in June, 1876. Not quite two months later Wild Bill Hickok had been murdered in the No. 10 Saloon. Never had any two men deserved less to be enshrined in the mythology of a nation. Yet, in an orgy of print, both of them had been immortalized in newspapers as well as books and periodicals. The general public accepted what it read as truth carved in stone. So it was that Custer and Hickok had achieved in death what they had vainly pursued in life—the glory of everlasting fame.

Sadder still were the unsung paladins of the frontier. The men who deserved public acclaim, men who actually were legend in their own time. Yet, because they shunned the limelight and sought no personal glory, their names were virtually unknown outside the western territories. Starbuck felt himself privileged to have met a few of them personally. Foremost in his mind were three peace officers of unquestionable courage: Tom Smith, Heck Thomas, and Dallas Stoudenmire. He was on his way now to meet yet another such lawman. A grizzled veteran by the name of Seth Bullock.

Starbuck made a leisurely tour of the Bad Lands. To all appearances, he was a gambler out surveying the prospects. Deadwood, the richest of all gold camps, was a magnet for the sporting crowd. The stakes were high, the play was fast, and suckers were soon parted from their money. The vice district was contained within a few square blocks, and there the action was nonstop, night and day. Whores, whiskey, and games of chance were the principal attractions. A man out to see the elephant saw it all in Deadwood.

While he walked, Starbuck searched his memory for everything he knew about Seth Bullock. Their acquaintance stemmed from his correspondence with peace officers throughout the West. He'd first written Bullock last year, selecting him for the best of all reasons. No better contact existed in Dakota Territory.

Seth Bullock was universally feared and respected by the outlaw element. He had served as a sheriff in Montana before joining the rush to Deadwood in '76. Upon arrival, he'd opened a hardware store, prospering as the boom got under way. Yet he was bothered by the lawlessness and violence of a raw mining camp. In league with other responsible citizens, he had organized a Board of Commissioners to police the town. Their first act was an ordinance restricting the vice district to lower Main Street. Their second act was the appointment of Bullock as sheriff, and with it a mandate to enforce the law. Within a year, he'd driven the outlaws out of Deadwood and convinced the sporting crowd to toe the line. In 1878, the territorial attorney general had secured his appointment to the post of U.S. deputy marshal. He was the law in Deadwood.

Over the years, Bullock had become a man of influence and prominence in Dakota Territory. After one term as sheriff, he'd devoted himself to various business enterprises. In addition to the hardware store, he invested in several mining ventures and established a cattle ranch on the Belle Fourche River. Yet, despite his wealth, he had retained his commission as a U.S. deputy marshal. He was one of that rare breed of men who served the law out of personal commitment and a sense of duty. He still risked his life chasing stage-coach robbers and murderers, and he'd acquired a fearsome reputation with a gun. He was the man to be reckoned with in the Black Hills.

Starbuck wanted advice and information. He nonetheless thought it wiser to approach Bullock in secret. Their association, should it become public knowledge, might very well affect the plan he'd mapped out. Accordingly, he went to the end of the Bad Lands district, then crossed to the opposite side of the street. He casually strolled back uptown, pausing now and then to check out a gambling dive. At the corner of Main and Wall, he stepped into the hardware store. A couple of clerks were busy waiting on customers, and paid him no notice. He browsed his way toward the rear of the store, moving slowly toward a door marked private. He knocked once and entered unannounced.

The man seated behind the desk was tall and lithely built. He had piercing gray eyes, a droopy mustache, and wild bushy eyebrows. His nose was hawklike, almost hooked, and his jawline slanted to a prominent chin. He held a pistol trained on Starbuck's belly button.

"You oughtn't to pop in on a man without an invite."

Starbuck stood rock-still. "You must be Seth Bullock."

"Who might you be?"

"Luke Starbuck."

"That a fact?" Bullock eyed his funereal attire.

"If you're Starbuck, how come you're tricked out like a tinhorn?"

"I'm working undercover," Starbuck told him. "I trailed a murderer here and thought you might be able to give me an assist."

"If you're who you say you are"—Bullock gave him a dark look—"what was the last thing I wrote you about?"

Starbuck smiled. "Your last letter was in reply to my inquiry about a bank robber, Jack O'Hara. You said he hadn't been reported in Dakota Territory."

"Well, I'll be damned!" Bullock holstered his pistol and rose with an outstretched hand. "It's a pleasure, Luke. I've been wanting to meet you for a long spell now."

"Same here." Starbuck accepted his handshake. "I would've telegraphed ahead, but it's too risky. The bird I'm after probably has ears all over town."

"Who'd he murder?"

"A lawyer in Denver."

"What's his name?"

"James Horn," Starbuck said slowly. "Alias Ira Lloyd."

"Never heard of either one."

"That figures," Starbuck remarked. "He's one cagey son-of-a-bitch."

"Sounds the least bit personal." Bullock motioned, then resumed his seat. "Grab yourself a chair and lay it out for me."

Starbuck sat down and took a moment to light a cheroot. Then he told Bullock the entire story. He skipped certain details about Hole-in-the-Wall, honoring his word to Mike Cassidy. Yet the salient points were covered in sum and substance. The link to the

Black Hills Land Company was underscored as the most vital lead in the case. He concluded with a physical description of James Horn.

"I put his age at twenty-seven," he noted. "Any of that ring a bell?"

Bullock's voice was troubled. "Skyrockets would be more like it."

"You know him?"

"Oh, hell, yes!" Bullock paused, jawline set in a scowl. "He goes by the name of John Eastlake."

"How long has he lived in Deadwood?"

"Since day one!" Bullock said with a grim smile. "He showed up the fall of '76 and started throwing money around like it was going out of style. Bought himself a whole batch of claims, and then he organized the land company. Today, he owns about half the real estate down in the sporting district, and he's the second or third biggest mine owner in town. So he's nobody to mess with unless you've got the goods."

"What's that supposed to mean?"

"Pretty obvious," Bullock speculated. "He tried to kill you and now you're set on returning the favor."

"So?"

"How'd you figure to do it?"

"Call him out," Starbuck said coldly. "Pick the time and show my hand—force him to fight?"

"Won't work!" Bullock waved the idea aside. "He knows you'd kill him. So why should he fight?"

"He'll fight before he'd let me expose him as a murderer!"

"What evidence you got that it was him who killed the lawyer?"

Starbuck looked surprised, then suddenly irritated. "None."

"You can't even prove for a fact that Eastlake is Horn—can you?"

"No." Starbuck's features were immobile. "Even if I could, it wouldn't change things. There's nobody left to testify against him . . . they're all dead."

"So that's that!" Bullock dusted his hands. "You call him out and he'll just laugh in your face. Then he waits till things cool down and hires himself another backshooter to get you. His kind don't never do their own dirty work! You ought to know that, Luke."

"Yeah, you're right." Starbuck gave him a bitter grin. "I guess I lost sight of that . . . took it too personal."

"Who wouldn't!" Bullock pursed his lips and nodded solemnly. "Course, there's more than one way to skin a cat."

Starbuck studied him a moment, eyes dark and vengeful. "I'm open to ideas."

"One thing I didn't mention." Bullock leaned forward, very earnest now. "Eastlake's a big muckamuck hereabouts in politics. There's talk that he's the bagman for Deadwood. I can't prove it, but the word's around if you listen close. He collects graft from the sporting crowd and funnels it to the governor."

"Why would the governor take graft?"

Bullock laughed without mirth. "Guess you never heard of Nehemiah Ordway. He's crooked as a barrel of snakes, always was! Some folks got fed up with it and organized a reform party. So now he's in a do-or-die fight to save his hide."

"Where does Horn come into it?"

"He don't want Deadwood reformed! That'd

undercut his political base, not to mention all the property he owns in the vice district. So him and the governor are thick as spit!"

"What's all that got to do with me?"

"You want Eastlake—Horn—don't you?"

"I'm still listening."

Bullock was suddenly very quiet, eyes boring into him. "I can't nail them, but you could. You're a pro at working undercover, and that's the only thing that'll turn the trick. You help me and we'll send 'em to prison till their teeth rot out!"

"I don't want Horn in prison." Starbuck's voice was edged. "I want him dead."

"Half a loaf's better than none," Bullock said shrewdly. "I know Dakota Territory from A to Zizzard, and I could steer you to all the skeletons. Course, along the way, you might get a crack at Eastlake. He'd likely fight if you threatened to bust his bubble here in Deadwood—destroy what he's built."

There was a prolonged silence. Starbuck rubbed his jawline and gazed off into space. He seemed to fall asleep with his eyes open, lost in some deep rumination. Presently he blinked, took a couple of quick puffs on his cheroot, and swung back to Bullock.

"You want the governor real bad, don't you?"

"Luke, just the thought of it makes my mouth water!"

"All right," Starbuck said with a clenched smile. "You got yourself a partner."

"All the way down the line . . . root hog or die?"

"All the way till the day we bury James Horn."

Chapter Sixteen

"Fifty simoleons!"

"Bump you a hundred."

"I fold."

"Too rich for my blood."

"I'm right behind you."

"Call the raise!"

Starbuck turned his hole card. "Three ladies."

"Bite my butt!" The miner who had called the raise tossed in three tens. "Pardee, it's a gawddamn good thing yore on the level. That kinda luck just ain't natural!"

"Luck's got nothing to do with it."

"Not that old chestnut!" the miner grumbled testily. "Poker ain't a game of chance, it's all skill—right?"

"Nope." Starbuck smiled, raking in the pot. "The secret's simpler than that . . . I pray a lot."

The other players whooped and jeered, and the miner mumbled something inaudible under his breath. Starbuck's mood was jovial and unruffled, the mark of a professional plying his trade. A gambling man always humored the losers and left them in a congenial frame of mind. He chuckled lightly at his own joke and began stacking the money on an already sizable pile of winnings. The next dealer gathered the cards and started shuffling.

The game was one of many under way in the Gem Theater. A combination saloon, gaming den, and brothel, the Gem was the most infamous dive in the Bad Lands. The owner, a loudmouthed slick named Al Swearingen, was something of an institution in Deadwood. His faro layouts and roulette tables were honest, and he served unwatered whiskey. Yet his square-deal policy stopped when it came to the bordello upstairs. He lured innocent girls out from the East, promising them stage jobs, and then converted them into dollar-a-trick whores. Everyone in town thought it all balanced out in the end. Honest games were preferable to cathouse morality.

Starbuck had made the Gem his unofficial headquarters. Over the past two weeks, he'd established himself as a gambler of some skill. He won consistently, working most of the dives in the Bad Lands, and he had made no enemies in the process. At the same time, he'd been at some pains to ingratiate himself with the sporting crowd. He was a free spender, quick to laugh, and always ready with a bawdy story. The man he'd cultivated more than any other was Al Swearingen. After hours, they frequently shared a bottle, and Swearingen had yet to realize he was being pumped for information. He considered Ace Pardee a prince of a fellow, one of the fraternity. And Starbuck slowly learned what made the wheels go round in Deadwood.

The dossier he'd put together on John Eastlake was now complete. The composite drawn was that of an ambitious man, who was at once munificent with his friends and ruthless with anyone who opposed his will. Yet he was noted as a man of character, scrupulous in all his business dealings, and a civic booster without rival. On the surface, he was dedicated to the greater good of the community and the advancement of his own burgeoning empire. Beneath the surface, however, there was a darker undercurrent. Unveiled there was the man inside—James Horn.

An astute entrepreneur, Horn exhibited foresight and a flair for organization. His intellect was demonstrated in the manner in which he'd structured his business empire. All his holdings were sheltered under the umbrella of the Black Hills Land Company, with a manager responsible for each division. He leased out his mining properties, thereby avoiding capital expenditure, and took a hefty cut of the profits in lieu of a fee, The proceeds were then plowed back into added mining ventures and the acquisition of real estate. The constant reinvestment and expansion had made him the most influential businessman in Deadwood. He owned pieces of two banks, a couple of hotels, and mining properties throughout every camp in the Black Hills. His real-estate holdings in the vice district were a veritable money tree. There, following the same formula employed in the mining division, he acted as a partner rather than a landlord. His cut was twenty percent straight off the top.

Payoffs for political graft were uncovered with remarkable ease. Operating openly, with uncanny sleight of hand, Horn simply integrated the payoffs into his vice-district revenues. The dives quartered in buildings he owned were visited once a week by a collector and two bruisers riding shotgun. The initial tipoff came from Al Swearingen, who tended to consume a good deal of his own liquor. Over a bottle one night—with Starbuck all ears—he bemoaned the payoffs, which, added to the twenty percent rental fee, were driving him to the poorhouse. Starbuck confirmed the lead by tailing the collector and his goons; their route covered the whole of the Bad Lands, every whorehouse, dance hall, and busthead saloon. Without exception, everyone shelled out, and Horn was clearly unworried by loose talk or legal repercussions. The reason was patently obvious.

Horn controlled the political apparatus of Lawrence County. His power base was Deadwood, the county seat, and the courthouse was his fiefdom. He operated behind the scenes, a shadowy kingfish who handpicked all candidates for office. Those he selected represented themselves as champions of the working man, decrying the excesses of wealthy mine owners and the business community. As a result, the coalition he'd put together was made up of beguiled miners and the sporting crowd, who voted a straight ticket every time out. Opposition had gradually withered, until now there was only token resistance when elections rolled around. From a practical standpoint, it had ceased to be a contest in Lawrence County. He owned the ballot box.

On a higher plane, Seth Bullock had enlightened Starbuck regarding territorial politics. Dakota was a stewpot of corruption and graft. Elected officials operated on the theory of enrichment through legislation, passing laws that lined their own pockets or generated kickbacks from vested interests. Legislators went to Yankton, the territorial capital, imbued not with honesty but with schemes for personal benefit. One newspaper editor, in a scathing editorial, indicted the lot: "We will match Dakota against all the world in ancient or modern times to produce as many official thieves and purchasable legislators."

The division of spoils was never better illustrated than in the frauds involving Indian reservations. Syndicates composed of merchants and legislators seized on the opportunity for economic exploitation. The Sioux were shortchanged on rations and forced to endure privations that bordered on genocide. The profits were astronomical, and the practice was widely condoned. A few Indians more or less rated small attention.

A greater concern in the political arena was the struggle over statehood. One faction believed Dakota should remain a ward of the federal govenment. A coalition of vested interests, such as the railroads, and Washington politicos, who controlled the purse strings, had joined with the governor to maintain territorial status. The opposition, intent on self-rule, believed Dakota should sever the cord and petition for statehood. Under the banner of the Dakota Citizens' League, its membership was a strange amalgamation of farmers, prohibitionists, and civic reformers. The battle was joined in the byways and corridors of the territorial capital.

Governor Nehemiah Ordway stood to lose the most if Dakota was granted statehood. Appointed to office two years ago, he had undertaken a Byzantine plan to create a vast political machine. Only after the fact, when it was much too late, did the opposition realize the full extent of his scheme. By controlling federal patronage, Ordway had established alliances with powerful leaders throughout Dakota. Not the least of those aligned with the governor was John Eastlake.

Statehood, in Eastlake's view, was bad for Deadwood and Lawrence County. Territorial status was a looser form of government, with less control exerted from Yankton. The county political apparatus, not to mention patronage jobs and public funds, was more easily managed when left in the hands of a few men. Then, too, the Dakota Citizens' League was the kiss of death for the wide-open mining camps of the Black Hills. Once reformers got control of Yankton, the whorehouses, saloons, and gaming dens would quickly become a thing of the past. In the end it boiled down to self-interest, and what was bad for Deadwood was equally bad for John Eastlake. He'd thrown his support to Governor Ordway.

Nor were the motives of Seth Bullock derived wholly from altruism. Starbuck had learned that the lawman was seeking revenge of a different sort. In the county elections of 1877, Bullock had been turned out of office as sheriff. His opponent had been backed by Horn, who at the time was making his first bid to assume the reins of power. In concert with Yankton politicians, Horn had engineered a stunning victory. Bullock, despite his reputation as a town tamer, went down to defeat. A proud man, he was also one who never forgave an affront. He considered Horn an enemy, and he was out to settle an old score. By toppling the governor, he would bring the political structure of Lawrence County tumbling into ruin. And leave Horn—John Eastlake—standing amidst the rubble.

Only one thing in the investigation had given Starbuck pause. By listening more than he talked, he'd uncovered a curious revelation. Some years ago Horn had married a refined eastern lady, who divorced him not six months after the wedding. There was speculation among the sporting crowd that she couldn't take the rough life of a mining camp. Yet there were other rumors afloat in the gossipy world of the Bad Lands. Horn reportedly had some kinky sex habits, involving leather straps and the infliction of pain. Among the whores of the vice district he was known as the Marquis de Eastlake. Starbuck was amused but hardly surprised. It was a window into Horn's character.

In subsequent days, it became apparent to Starbuck that he'd done all the spadework possible in Deadwood. There was nothing of any substance left to learn about Horn and the local political ring. Nor was anything unearthed to date particularly incriminating in itself. He had devoted considerable thought to the problem, and he always returned to the graft payoffs. It seemed unlikely Horn would entrust the transfer of the money to anyone else; the fewer witnesses the better when illegal funds were passing hands. Then, too, Bullock had told him that Horn made periodic trips to Yankton, generally once a month. So he saw only one recourse, the logical next step. He must somehow tie Horn and the graft payoffs to Governor Nehemiah Ordway.

The plan he evolved was larded with risk. Horn most certainly had his photograph, and might very well see through his disguise. Over the past two weeks, all quite unobtrusively, he had observed Horn from a distance. On one occasion he had loitered across from the land company, and on another he had discreetly tailed Horn through the business district. Yet he'd cautiously avoided any face-to-face meeting. As a result, his disguise had never been tested. That worried him more than he cared to admit.

While it was extreme, there seemed no alternative to shadowing Horn on his next trip to Yankton. Only in that manner could he establish a direct link to the governor. The stage ride to the territorial capital took several days, and he would be caged with Horn inside the coach the entire time. The chance of being recognized was not to be discounted; even a slip of the tongue could destroy his cover. Still, however calculated the risk, the option was to sit on his thumb and do nothing. He was determined to see the case through, and he at last made the decision to go for broke. Ace Pardee would accompany Horn to Yankton.

There were two stages a day to the capital. One departed early in the morning and the other at noon. The date of Horn's next trip, and which stage he would board, were known only to Horn himself. So Starbuck hedged his bet by arising every morning at the crack of dawn. He would then stroll casually past the stage line shortly before departure time. The ploy was repeated again at noon, always with a quick visual check of the passengers. Finally, on the morning of the fourth day, he got a break. As he stepped out of the hotel, he spotted Horn walking along the street, suitcase in hand. He hurried back to his room, collected his valise, and settled accounts with the desk clerk. Then he made a beeline for the stage office.

Purchasing a ticket was the first test. Horn was waiting outside with several other passengers, standing somewhat apart. He glanced in Starbuck's direction, then his eyes moved on. Encouraged, Starbuck went inside and paid the fare to Yankton. When he emerged, the passengers were already in the process of boarding. He hoisted himself into the coach and took the only vacant seat, directly across from Horn. A few moments later the luggage was loaded and the driver popped his whip over the rumps of the six-horse hitch. The stage began the long climb out of Deadwood gulch.

The morning passed uneventfully. The passengers were for the most part drummers and businessmen. Some caught a catnap while others talked quietly as the coach jounced and swayed through the mountains. If Horn knew any of them, it was not apparent by his actions. He made no attempt to join in the conversation, and none of the men addressed him directly. He sat wrapped in silence, withdrawn into the privacy of his own thoughts. His visage was meditative.

Starbuck felt as though he were in the presence of a dead man. What seemed a lifetime ago—after he'd infiltrated the gang of horse thieves—he had once spoken briefly with Dutch Henry Horn. The recollection was vivid, and today it was as if he found himself seated across from a specter. Horn was the very image of his father, both in looks and in manner. There was something impenetrable about him, an aura of personal insensitivity. His composure was monumental, and he seemed not just aloof but genuinely comfortable with his own company. Only his eyes moved, alert and penetrating, the color of carpenter's chalk. He stared out at the countryside, his mouth a tight gashlike line. He looked every bit as dangerous as his father.

On the outskirts of Rapid City, the stage stopped for a late noon meal. While a fresh team was being hitched, the passengers trooped inside the relay station. The meal consisted of fried fat pork, beans and biscuits, and muddy coffee. Starbuck avoided Horn, taking a place at the opposite end of the table. After the meal, however, there was no way to keep his distance. Courtesy of the road dictated that each passenger resume his original seat. When the stage pulled out, they were once more across from each other. He slowly became aware that Horn was covertly watching him.

A mile or so out of town, Horn suddenly faced him directly. The full impact of his strange, dispassionate gaze was unsettling. His features were expressionless.

"Have we met?" he asked. "You look familiar."

"Don't think so." Starbuck went into his tinhorn routine. "Course, we could've bumped into one another at the Gem. I hang out there pretty regular."

"Then you must know Al Swearingen?"

"Why, sure thing!" Starbuck said with dazzling good humor. "Al's the salt of the earth, none better! He a friend of yours too, Mr.—?"

"Eastlake." Horn smiled without warmth. "Swearingen's a business acquaintance, not a friend. I take it you're a gambler?"

"Bet your boots!" Starbuck hooked his thumbs in his vest, grinned broadly. "Ace Pardee's the name and poker's my game. Open for business six days a week and all day on Sunday!"

Horn regarded him with an odd, steadfast look. "Are you new to Deadwood, Mr. Pardee?"

Starbuck sensed it was no idle question. For all the dyed hair and eyepatch, Horn clearly detected some similarity to his photo. He nerved himself to give a sterling performance.

"Got in a couple of weeks ago," he said affably. "By way of Frisco and points west."

"What brings you to Dakota Territory?"

"The root of all evil!" Starbuck boomed out jovially. "Heard there was gold in them thar hills! And I'll tell you true, Mr. Eastlake"—he lowered his one eyelid in a sly wink—"it surely weren't no rumor!"

"I thought a gambler never quit a winner."

"Don't believe I exactly follow you?"

"If Deadwood's so lucrative," Horn inquired in a reasonable tone, "why travel all the way to Yankton?"

Starbuck laughed a wild braying laugh. "You're not a politician, are you, Mr. Eastlake?"

"No," Horn said shortly. "Why do you ask?"

"I heard there's a freeze-out game in Yankton. Some of them crooked legislators and fat-cat railroad boys are gonna shoot for the moon! Figured I'd go have a look-see."

"You don't say?"

"Well, I don't say it too loud!" Starbuck uttered a roguish chuckle. "I wouldn't want to warn 'em Ace Pardee's on his way!"

Horn abruptly lost interest. "I wish you luck, Mr. Pardee."

"Say, looky here now!"

Starbuck produced a deck of cards from his inside coat pocket. He deftly shuffled on his knees and gave the deck a smooth one-handed cut. The other passengers were spellbound by his dexterity, and sat watching him with the expression normally reserved for sword swallowers. He riffled the cards with a flourish and gave them a come-on grin.

"Why wait till Yankton!" he said with a gleam in his eye. "Anybody play the game of poker?"

A couple of the drummers and one of the businessmen allowed themselves to be talked into a game. With a valise balanced on their knees, they hunched forward and a hand of stud was quickly dealt. Horn looked on with icy detachment for a moment, then went back to staring out the window. Starbuck suppressed a laugh and turned his attention to the cards.

He knew he'd passed the test.

Chapter Seventeen

John Eastlake spent two days in Yankton. He registered at the Dakota Hotel and went about his business in an open manner. No effort was made to conceal either his movements or the purpose of his trip.

Upon arrival, Starbuck checked into a seedy hotel across town. A nearby pawnshop, which sold used clothing, provided him with an outfit for yet another disguise. He chose a suit one size too large, a pair of worn brogans, and a battered slouch hat. The eyepatch and spit-curl mustache were retired to his valise, and replaced with a scraggly black beard. Though fake, the beard was a theatrical prop, crafted of real hair and genuine in appearance. To complete the masquerade, he adopted a shuffling gait and the stooped posture of a man aged by hard times. He looked very much the ragtag tramp.

Posing as a panhandler, Starbuck was all but invisible in the hustle and bustle of downtown Yankton. He shadowed Horn day and night, easily melding into the background. As John Eastlake, the Deadwood kingfish, Horn was warmly received by the political oligarchy. On the first day, he met with a succession of legislators from around the territory. Early the second morning he went to the capitol and met privately with Governor Nehemiah Ordway. There was no attempt at secrecy, and to all indications his meeting with the governor was by appointment. His business accomplished, he then returned to the hotel and checked out. He boarded the afternoon stage for Deadwood.

Starbuck was left in a maze of doubt. His surveillance had uncovered nothing incriminating and no hint of corruption. Nor was any damaging inference to be drawn from the meetings. Businessmen and lobbyists were constantly seeking favors from both the governor and members of the legislature. John Eastlake was simply one of a very large crowd.

Further obscured was the matter of graft. There was every reason to believe that Horn, in his meeting with the governor, had passed along the payoffs from Deadwood's sporting district. Yet there was no proof—nor any glimmer of an eyewitness—that money had actually exchanged hands. In short, there was no evidence of illegality and no way to substantiate the existence of corrupt practices. The surveillance, start to finish, was a washout.

Following Horn's departure, Starbuck was somewhat at a loss. He returned to his hotel room and flopped down on the bed. Hands locked behind his head, he stared at the ceiling in a brooding funk. His investigation had run up against a stone wall, and he saw no way to surmount the problem. Horn was on cordial terms with the governor and a gaggle of legislators, and clearly no stranger to the corridors of the capitol. Still, for all his high-placed connections, there was no crime involved. The business of Dakota Territory, as everyone readily admitted, was politics. Horn appeared as legitimate as the next man.

Starbuck nonetheless saw it through a prism of his own attitude. In his experience, those who tended the vineyards of government were by nature the worst of all bloodsuckers. He marked again that venal men in a political marketplace were corrupted by a system that thrived on skullduggery. Some men were corrupted by ambition and a thirst for power, and others were merely creatures of their own avarice. Almost all of them, however, were some strain of parasite. The few who weren't inevitably suffered a fate similar to that of the original reformer. The mob spiked them to a cross.

All of which served to infuriate Starbuck even further. There seemed little likelihood he would preside over the crucifixion of James Horn. Without hard evidence, his investigation was scotched and his odyssey of nearly two months was at a standstill. He had the sensation of a man sinking ever deeper into quicksand. He was going nowhere but down.

By late afternoon, he'd muddled the impasse from every angle. No workable plan presented itself, and a sort of sluggish pessimism crept over him. Then, ever so slowly, the germ of an idea took shape. The thought occurred that Horn would never entrust his well-being into the hands of other men. Nor would he hazard his fate to the vicissitudes of the political arena. Power brokers were forever jockeying for position, and today's alliances were as ephemeral as a zephyr. When crooks parted ways, only a fine line separated the oxes from the foxes. Someone was always thrown to the mob, a sacrificial offering. And James Horn was not a man to get caught with his pants down.

One thought led to another in rapid sequence.

Any equation involving Horn and political survival translated into only one possible answer: blackmail. The man had the character of an assassin and all the social virtues of a scorpion. In the event of political upheaval, he would emerge the high priest, the one who performed the sacrifice. To guarantee that outcome, it followed he would have some form of leverage, an insurance policy. Whatever the nature of that insurance, several things were beyond speculation. It would be in writing, documentation of some sort that would provide evidence of graft and corruption. Moreover, it would indict a wide spectrum of politicians, most especially the governor of Dakota Territory. A man with all that need never fear exposure, for the mere threat of blackmail would insure his own impunity. James Horn was just such a man.

The premise seemed to Starbuck almost a lead-pipe cinch. He sat bolt upright in bed, concentrating hard. The only questions that remained were where, and how, he might lay his hands on Horn's insurance policy. He thought he knew where to look.

Hurrying out of the hotel, he walked directly to the train depot. He scribbled a short message to Verna Phelps, and passed it through the window to the station telegrapher. The wire was cryptic, worded in a code known only to himself and Verna. When deciphered, it read simply:

CONTACT TYRONE QUINN. HIRE HIM FOR A BLIND JOB AND PUT HIM ON THE FIRST TRAIN TO YANKTON.
STARBUCK

The telegrapher evidenced no great curiosity. He was accustomed to secret messages in the convoluted world of Dakota politics, and toted up the charge without a word. Starbuck waited while he hunched over his key and tapped out the wire. A schedule posted on the wall provided information on routes and arrival times. By way of Denver, there was only one connection to Yankton. Tyronne Quinn would arrive day after tomorrow.

Outside, Starbuck lit a cigar and strolled back uptown. He was confident Verna would handle the chore with dispatch and efficiency. He was equally certain Tyrone Quinn would accept the job without hesitation. He made a practice of obligating members of the Denver underworld, and only last year he'd saved Quinn from a long term in prison. The man was incorrigible, a professional thief and master safecracker. But when the marker was called, a professional always paid his debts. Quinn would be on the train.

Looking ahead, Starbuck formulated a loose plan. Time and distance were the critical factors, and he proceeded on the assumption Quinn would arrive in Yankton as scheduled. In that event, they would then board the stage for Deadwood the following morning. To all appearances, they would be fellow gamblers, traveling to the mecca of the Black Hills. By the end of the week they would pull into Deadwood, and the weekend seemed the perfect time for the job. Horn's land-company office would be closed on Sunday, so that made Sunday night the target date. Some inner hunch told him the office safe, rather than Horn's home, was the place to look. As to the safe itself, he foresaw no problems. Quinn would open it like a tin of sardines.

Which made Monday the day of reckoning. Between now and then, assuming the safe divulged.

Horn's secrets, he would decide on the next step. He figured there were a couple of options, one of them involving Seth Bullock.

The other was strictly lone hand . . . all the way.

It was late evening. Gold Street was empty, gripped in a weblike darkness. A pale sickle moon dimly lighted the sky, and streetlamps flickered at the corner of Main. The sound of a raucous Sunday-night crowd carried distinctly from the Bad Lands.

Starbuck kept watch on the distant intersection. Tyrone Quinn took a locksmith's pick from his vest pocket and inserted its slim, flat tip into the door lock. Gingerly, working by feel, he probed and tested; within seconds there was a soft *click*. He replaced the pick in his pocket and turned the doorknob. Without a word, they stepped inside the Black Hills Land Company. Quinn swiftly closed and locked the door.

A moment passed while Starbuck studied the layout of the outer office. Then he led the way to a door on the far side of the room. There seemed little question it was the entrance to Horn's inner sanctum; a double set of locks had been installed in the door. Quinn went to work with his flat-nosed pick and the door quickly swung open.

The office was furnished with good taste. A large desk dominated the room, and grouped before it were three wingback chairs. Along the near wall was a leather sofa and the floor was carpeted. Yet, for all the expensive furnishings, security was quite plainly the overriding consideration. There were no windows, and the double-locked door was the only entrance. On the far wall stood a massive steel safe.

Closing the door, Quinn moved directly to the

safe. A candle and a round metal disk appeared from his inside jacket pocket. While Starbuck watched, he struck a match and lit the candle. The snuffed match was returned to his pocket; he dripped hot wax on the metal disk and sealed the butt of the candle firmly in place. Expertly, he examined the safe, all the time muttering to himself. At last, he set the candle on the floor and knelt down. He glued one ear to the safe door and briskly rubbed his hands together. Then he began rotating the combination knob.

Tyrone Quinn possessed a magic touch. Somewhat esthetic in appearance, he was short and wiry, with the watery eyes of a sparrow. His hands were delicate, the fingers smooth and tapered. He oiled them daily with glycerine and before a job he lightly sandpapered the finger pads to create a sensitive feel no less acute than antennae. Tonight, his fingers were alive, the nerve endings like exquisite sensors. It took only seven minutes until the last tumbler rolled into position.

Quinn smiled, and rose to his feet. "Any idea when your man was born?"

"No," Starbuck said shortly. "What the hell's that got to do with anything?"

"A matter of curiosity," Quinn replied in a reedy voice. "The combination is left 5—right 12—left 55. If he's twenty-seven, then that's when he was born. Lots of people use their birthdate as a combination . . . it helps 'em to remember."

"Let's get on with it."

Quinn shrugged and turned the handle on the safe. Then he opened the double doors and stepped aside. Candlelight revealed several rows of shelves at the top and a large storage area at the bottom. Star-

buck moved to the safe and began his search with the
topmost shelf. The material he found was largely confidential files and accounting ledgers relating to the
land company. On the last shelf were stacks of cash
totaling something less than two thousand dollars.
Hidden behind the money was a Colt double-action
revolver. He turned his attention to the bottom storage
area.

Outdated ledgers and files stuffed with old correspondence occupied most of the space. After paw-
ing through it item by item, he suddenly stopped and
leaned forward. He reached deep into the safe and
pulled from the rear a wide leather satchel. Opening
the clasp, he took out a small ledger and flipped
through the pages. Listed there, with a page for every
dive in the Bad Lands, were entries representing the
graft collections. One column of figures noted the
amount collected; a second column, calculated to
the penny, represented seventy-five percent of the total. Neatly lettered above the second column was the
name ORDWAY, and the conclusion was obvious.
The governor got the lion's share for his political war
chest. The balance, a full twenty-five percent, was
skimmed off the top by James Horn. Quite probably,
it went to fund his county organization.

Starbuck dug farther into the satchel. Whatever
he expected, he was amazed by what he found. Horn
had gathered incontestable documentation on the governor's corrupt practices. An affidavit by the publisher
of the Deadwood *Sentinel* indicated Ordway had organized a wide-ranging conspiracy among the territory's newspapers. Government printing contracts,
which represented a substantial volume of business,
had been awarded to a select group of publishers. In

return, the newspapers supported Ordway and voiced his political sentiments in all press coverage. The effect was a propaganda machine of staggering proportions.

Other documents revealed that patronage had been used in a criminal manner. Ordway, as territorial governor, was empowered to appoint county commissioners throughout Dakota. An affidavit from a Lawrence County commissioner indicated Ordway had transformed patronage into a scheme to line his own pockets. The appointments were conducted somewhat like an auction, with the office going to the highest bidder. The commissioners, moreover, served at the governor's pleasure. He could remove them from office as quickly as he had appointed them. The result was a stranglehold on the men who dispensed government funds at the county level. Ordway owned every commissioner throughout the whole Dakota Territory.

Starbuck was grimly amused by his discovery. The contents of the satchel were indeed an insurance policy. Horn, with one stroke, could send the governor and a phalanx of county commissioners to federal prison. The conspiracy with newspaper publishers, while not so serious, was also an indictable offense. Whether or not the affidavits had been obtained by coercion was a moot point. In a court of law they would prove irrefutable, and reduce the political structure of Dakota to a shambles. Despite himself, Starbuck felt a grudging sense of admiration. Horn was a crafty infighter, and he played for keeps.

Hefting the satchel, Starbuck turned toward the door. Quinn closed the safe and spun the combination knob. The candle was extinguished and returned to the safe-cracker's pocket. On the way out, both the door to Horn's office and the street door were once more locked. There was no sign of their entry and nothing was disturbed. The job had consumed not quite an hour.

Starbuck was silent as they walked toward the corner. Then, nearing the intersection, he glanced sideways at Quinn. His eyes were stony.

"I want you on the morning stage to Cheyenne. Take the train from there to Denver."

Quinn bobbed his head. "Whatever you say, Luke."

"One last thing," Starbuck said flatly. "You never heard of Deadwood or the Black Hills Land Company, Savvy?"

"Never fear!" Quinn laughed nervously. "Mum's the word!"

"I'll hold you to it," Starbuck warned him. "Don't let me hear any rumors floating around the Tenderloin when I get home."

Quinn understood perfectly. Only the bare details of the job had been revealed to him, and he had no idea whose safe he'd just cracked. Nor was he interested in pursuing the matter further. He owed a debt and he'd paid off, and that was that. Silence was part of the bargain, not so much professional courtesy as common good sense. For he also understood his life was forfeit if he developed a loose lip. Starbuck tolerated no man who broke an agreement, and there was no court of appeal. The verdict stood.

At the corner, they stopped in a pool of light from the streetlamp. Starbuck was once again in the guise of Ace Pardee. The black eyepatch and the mustache intrigued Quinn, but he wisely suppressed his curiosity. He'd asked no questions over the past several days and he asked none now. All he knew about Starbuck's work was what he read in the papers, and that was all he wanted to know. A mankiller who operated undercover was best left to his own secrets.

"I'm obliged, Tyrone." Starbuck extended his hand. "You haven't lost your touch."

"It's a gift," Quinn said modestly, pumping his arm. "I play tumblers the way some people play a piano. We all have our calling."

"Maybe so." Starbuck let go his hand. "Just make sure you hear the call for the Cheyenne stage."

"Why, I wouldn't miss it for the world! No, indeed, I surely wouldn't!"

Quinn waved and walked off in the direction of the hotel. Starbuck watched him a moment, then turned downstreet. From the Bad Lands, he heard laughter and shouts, and the discordant blare of a brass band. Sunday night was always a big night in the sporting district, and he saw throngs of miners on the boardwalk outside the dives. Uptown was deserted, and a look around revealed he had the street to himself. His pace quickened.

A block farther on he approached Seth Bullock's hardware store. At the corner, he paused and slowly inspected the street in both directions. There was no one in sight, but he took a moment longer to scan the darkened doorways of shops and businesses. Then, satisfied he wasn't being followed, he turned onto Wall Street. The lamplight faded and he moved through the night to the rear of the building.

He ducked into the alleyway behind Bullock's store.

Chapter Eighteen

Early the next morning Starbuck left his hotel and walked toward Gold Street. His mood was somber, and he scarcely noticed passersby as he reflected on the problem at hand. He was absorbed with thoughts of mortality.

Outside the land company he paused and squared his shoulders. Then he opened the door and entered with a determined stride. He halted in the outer office, assessing the situation at a glance. Several clerks were seated at their desks, and three partitioned cubicles were ranged along the front wall. The men inside the cubbyholes were quickly identified as the managers of Horn's various enterprises. He grinned broadly and nodded to the nearest clerk.

"I'd like to see Mr. Eastlake."

"Oh?" The clerk gave his tinhorn attire and the eyepatch a swift once-over. "Is he expecting you, Mr.—?"

"Ace Pardee," Starbuck replied jovially. "Your boss told me to drop around anytime."

"Well, in that case, I'll just inform—"

"No need for ceremony! I'll announce myself."

Starbuck laughed with hearty good cheer. Before the clerk could move, he quickly crossed the room to the unmarked door. Throwing it open, he plastered a wide smile on his face and stepped into Horn's office.

"Hullo there, Mr. Eastlake!"

Horn jumped, shoving away from his desk. He rose partway out of his chair, then resumed his seat as Starbuck closed the door. His features took on a guarded look.

"How was Yankton, Mr. Pardee?"

"Broke the game!" Starbuck said ebulliently. "Walked away with all the marbles and then some!"

"Congratulations." Horn's face was blank, his eyes opaque. "What can I do for you?"

"Thought we might talk a little business."

Horn stared at him. "Business?"

"Political business." Starbuck lowered himself into one of the wing chairs, pulled out a cheroot. "Turns out we've got some mutual acquaintances."

"I see." Horn regarded him thoughtfully. "Are you referring to the poker game in Yankton . . . the legislators you trimmed?"

"Nope." Starbuck lit up and puffed a cottony wad of smoke. "I was thinking of Nehemiah Ordway."

"Ordway?" Horn stiffened, fully alert. "What interest do you have in the governor?"

"Well, for openers"—Starbuck studied the tip of his cigar—"you and him swill at the same trough."

Horn sat perfectly still. "I suggest you explain yourself, Mr. Pardee."

"All in good time." Starbuck casually flicked an ash onto the carpet. "I learned something else while I was in Yankton."

"I warn you, Mr. Pardee!" Horn's features set in a grim scowl. "I don't like being toyed with."

"Why, perish the thought!" Starbuck said smoothly.

"I just figured you'd want to know everything I know."

"Very well." Horn folded his hands, eased back in his chair. "I'm listening."

"The Dakota Hotel," Starbuck observed. "The one you stayed at in Yankton? I bribed the night clerk."

"I fail to see your point."

"Oh, it's a doozy! He let me have a gander at the hotel register. A few months ago—early May, to be exact—you and William Dexter were there at the same time."

"Dexter?" Horn seemed turned to stone. "I'm not familiar with the name."

Starbuck laughed in his face, "Suppose I jiggle your memory! There are bank records in Denver that tie you to Dexter. Once a month, he transferred funds from the Grubstake mine to the Black Hills Land Company. Get the picture now?"

"Go on."

"You killed Dexter, and you cleaned out his office files. But you overlooked the bank, and that's where I made the connection. Dexter was your number-one errand boy."

Horn's mouth clamped in a bloodless line. "Who are you?"

"Starbuck." A slow, dark smile creased Starbuck's features. "Luke Starbuck."

"I—" Horn paused, jolted into sudden awareness. "I thought it was you, that day on the stage. You're to be commended, Mr. Starbuck. You fooled me completely."

"That makes us even," Starbuck said with a note

of irony. "You had me fooled from the day Dexter hired me."

"Hired you?" Horn said a bit too quickly. "I know nothing of any such arrangement."

"Come off it!" Starbuck brushed aside the objection. "You did your damnedest to get me killed. I can quote it to you chapter and verse! Mike Cassidy and Hole-in-the-Wall, the smoke screen in Butte. You name it and I've got the goods."

"Indeed?" Horn tensed, his expression watchful. "Why would I want to have you killed?"

"You're James Horn," Starbuck said with a clenched smile. "Your father was Dutch Henry Horn. Want me to go on?"

"I'm impressed, Mr. Starbuck. Your reputation as a detective apparently has some basis in fact."

"What's a fact," Starbuck said firmly, "is that I've got you by the short hairs."

"I think not," Horn countered. "There's nothing to connect me to Dexter's death, and no proof I attempted to have you killed. In case you've forgotten, you shot all the witnesses, Mr. Starbuck."

"You're a little slow," Starbuck pointed out. "I'm talking about politics, not murder."

"Oh, yes!" Horn gave him a quizzical look. "You did mention the governor, didn't you?"

"The governor and graft payoffs, and a wholesale market in patronage."

"Would you care to be more specific?"

"Ordway has seven newspapers—including the Deadwood *Sentinel*—locked into a conspiracy. They all dance to his tune."

"I doubt it seriously."

"He also controls every county commissioner in

the territory. And they all paid through the nose before he'd confirm their appointment."

"Unfounded rumors!" Horn advised loftily. "No one would believe a word of it!"

"Yeah, they will," Starbuck said with conviction. "I sort of accidentally-on-purpose stumbled across the proof."

"How interesting," Horn replied with cold hauteur. "Exactly what does that have to do with me, Mr. Starbuck?"

"I mentioned graft payoffs a minute ago."

"And?"

"You're the bagman for Deadwood."

"Absurd!" Horn announced. "A total fabrication!"

"Wanna bet?" Starbuck's eyes hooded. "I cracked your safe last night."

Horn's face went chalky. "You're lying!"

"Wrong again," Starbuck said woodenly. "I got the affidavits and the ledger that shows the split between you and Ordway on the graft. It's all I need to send you up for ten, maybe twenty years."

"I still say you're bluffing!"

"One way to find out." Starbuck motioned toward the safe. "The combination is left 5—right 12—left 55."

There was a moment of stunned silence. Then Horn rose from his chair and crossed the room. He approached the safe in the manner of a condemned man mounting the gallows. Dropping to one knee, he quickly spun the combination knob and heaved open the doors. A brief search of the storage compartment convinced him the affidavits and the ledger were missing. All the color drained from his face and his eyes dulled, appeared to turn inward. His head felt queer, almost as though his eardrums were blocked, and his brow glistened with beads of sweat. Finally, with his back still to Starbuck, he bowed his head and placed one hand on the lower shelf. His voice was shaky.

"Why haven't you gone to Bullock? You have the proof."

"I was tempted to do that very thing. Then, on second thought, I figured the marshal could wait."

"Don't mock me!" Horn said sharply. "Why are you here?"

"Guess."

"You intend to kill me, don't you?"

"Yeah, I do," Starbuck said simply. "I reckon I wouldn't sleep nights . . . even with you in prison."

"You fool!" Horn said with raw hatred. "It won't end here. Kill me and you're a dead man for certain!"

"I'll chance it."

Horn could scarcely mistake the finality of the statement. The death knell had sounded, and he was a doomed man. It flashed through his mind that he had nothing to lose. He could submit and die on his knees. Or he could try and yet live.

His hand brushed past the stacks of money and clutched the hidden revolver. He twisted around, still on one knee. He awkwardly banged his arm on the door of the safe, almost lost his balance. Then a look of stark terror suddenly crossed his features. He froze.

Starbuck was on his feet, waiting. The Colt six-gun was extended at arm's length, and there was a metallic whir as he thumbed the hammer. An instant of tomblike stillness slipped past while they stared at each other. Then he smiled and fired.

The slug drilled through Horn's forehead. The top of his skull exploded, blown off in a misty spray of brains and gore. He toppled over, driven backward by the impact, and fell wedged inside the safe. One leg kicked, his bootheel drumming the floor in afterdeath. His eyes rolled upward, then a wheezing rattle escaped his throat and he lay still.

Starbuck felt nothing. The man had tried repeatedly to kill him, and would have tried again. Whatever else he was, the son of Dutch Henry Horn was no quitter. One day, somewhere down the line, there would have been a time of retribution. So, in the end, it was kill or get killed. Which made it the simplest of all choices.

Only one emotion touched Starbuck. He was glad James Horn was dead. And somehow relieved, almost sanguine. It had been a long hunt.

Nor was he yet out of the woods. He moved to the door and flung it open. The men in the outer office were on their feet, their faces taut with apprehension. He leveled the sixgun and they hastily cleared a path. No one spoke as he crossed the room; his eyes and the Colt swept constantly from side to side. Once past the row of desks, he turned and kept them covered as he backed to the door. He stepped outside and holstered his pistol. Then he hurried toward the corner.

On Main Street, Starbuck turned downtown. He strode rapidly in the direction of Bullock's store, located on the next corner. The business district was already bustling with activity, and throngs of people jammed the boardwalk. Weaving in and out, he snaked through the crowd, ignoring the stares of passersby. When he was halfway down the block, a sudden shout behind him brought everything on the street to a standstill. He glanced over his shoulder and saw one of the land-company clerks standing at the corner. The shout became a shrill scream, wild and frenzied.

"Stop that man! He murdered Mr. Eastlake!"

Starbuck broke into a headlong sprint. Deadwood was infamous for vigilante justice, and the man known as John Eastlake was the town's leading citizen. In the hands of a mob, he knew he would be lynched without trial or hearing. He bulled past a hard-faced miner who attempted to block his path. Then he jerked the sixgun and wiggled the barrel with a menacing gesture. The crowd split apart, some hugging the walls of buildings and others scattering into the street. He took the last few steps and darted into the hardware store. He kept the Colt trained on the door.

Seth Bullock rushed forward from his office. Outside, a clot of townspeople quickly gathered on the boardwalk, and more came running. Word spread along the street like wildfire, and there was a buzz of excitement mingled with dark mutterings. Bullock halted beside him, one eye on the crowd. His face was etched with bewilderment.

"What the hell's all that about?"

"I braced Horn," Starbuck said stolidly. "He went for a gun and I killed him."

"Holy Jesus!" Bullock cursed. "Get on back to my office and lock the door."

"I'd sooner take my chances here."

"Don't argue! I want you out of sight—now!"

Starbuck hesitated, then slowly backed toward the rear of the store. Bullock grabbed a shotgun off a nearby rack and emptied a box of shells on the counter. He swiftly loaded both barrels and snapped the breech closed. Then he walked to the door and stopped, the scattergun centered on the mob. His voice was harsh, commanding.

"Clear out! The man's my prisoner and I've got a load of buckshot for anybody that disagrees. Go on, gawddamnit—get moving!"

The shotgun was steady, and the barrels looked big as mine shafts. The crowd stared back at him a moment; then those in the front rank turned away. The movement broke the spell and the mob dispersed to the opposite side of the street. Bullock slammed the door and locked it. His eyes were grim as he walked toward the office.

While Bullock listened, Starbuck briefly recounted the events of the past two days. He outlined how the safe had been cracked and explained in some detail the ledger dealing with graft collections. For reasons of his own, he omitted any mention of the affidavits linking Governor Ordway to political corruption. He concluded with a straightforward account of Horn's death.

"Thought so," Bullock said when he finished. "You went there plannin' to kill him, didn't you?"

"What's the difference?" Starbuck replied. "He's dead and that ends it. All I want now is a ticket out of Deadwood."

"How d'you figure to do that? The sheriff and the whole courthouse crowd were Horn's stooges. You'll be charged with murder sure as thunder!"

"I've got something to trade."

"Yeah?" Bullock eyed him narrowly. "What's that?"

"The ledger," Starbuck said with a tired smile. "It indicts the courthouse crowd the same as it did Horn.

What's in there could send every last one of them to prison. I'll swap it for a ticket on the Cheyenne stage."

"God a'mighty!" Bullock glowered at him in tongue-tied rage. "That'd let Ordway off the hook too! We wouldn't have a case against nobody!"

"No way around it, Seth." Starbuck gave him a downcast look. "It's that or they'll have me decorating a tree by sundown."

"You rigged it!" Bullock said with sudden understanding. "You rigged it so you could kill Horn and walk away clean! All the time you wasn't thinkin' about nobody but yourself!"

"You believe what you want to believe. It doesn't change a thing."

"Where's the ledger?"

"Hidden," Starbuck said evasively. "I'll tell you where after the coroner's inquest."

"What inquest?"

"That's the rest of the deal." A wintry smile lighted Starbuck's eyes. "I want the whole story on the record. Horn's real identity, and how he tried to have me assassinated. And I want a coroner's jury to clear me of killing him—all neat and official and in writing!"

"You really think a bunch of politicians are gonna buy that? Hell, they'll probably figure you're tryin' to set 'em up for a double-cross!"

"No inquest, no ledger," Starbuck said equably. "I don't see they've got any choice."

Bullock chewed at his mustache before answering. "Why should I go out of my way to make your deal? You've done spoilt my game all to hell and gone!"

"Trust me, Seth." Starbuck stared straight into his gaze. "You won't regret it."

Silence thickened between them. Finally, with a great shrug of resignation, Bullock cleared his throat. "Guess I couldn't rightly let 'em stretch your neck. I'll go see what we can work out."

After the lawman was gone, Starbuck locked the door and fired up a cheroot. He took a chair, puffing smoke, and propped his boots on the desk. He looked pleased as a tomcat spitting feathers.

The stagecoach stood outside the Deadwood station. To the east, the sun crested the mountains like a fiery globe. Several passengers were milling about, awaiting the call to board. Their destination was Cheyenne.

Starbuck and Bullock were off to one side, talking quietly. The coroner's inquest, held yesterday afternoon, had created a sensation. Starbuck's testimony regarding John Eastlake's true identity had turned the town topsy-turvy. The assassination plot, corroborated by Bullock, had put the final onus on the dead man. The verdict was justifiable homicide, and the news had been flashed to papers all across the territory. The courthouse crowd, having fulfilled their end of the bargain, had spent an uneasy night. One piece of business still remained.

Squinting into the sun, Starbuck lowered his voice. "You know that loading dock out behind your store?"

"In the alley?" Bullock cocked his head. "What about it?"

"Dig down a foot or so over at the left side. You'll find a leather satchel buried there. The ledger's inside."

"Well, I'll be damned!"

"You'll find something else, too." A slow smile tugged at the corner of Starbuck's mouth. "There's a couple of affidavits that ought to put Ordway on the rockpile till he's an old man."

Bullock looked astounded. "Affidavits about what?"

"When you've read them, you'll understand. I'd suggest you go have a talk with the attorney general. Once he's empaneled a grand jury and issued subpoenas, the lid will blow sky high. There'll be all kinds of newspaper publishers and county commissioners ready to turn songbird."

"Newspaper—"

"Not so loud!" Starbuck cut him short. "Just read the affidavits. You'll hang Ordway, and along with him your own courthouse crowd. There's plenty of rope for everybody."

Bullock considered briefly, then nodded. "How come you didn't tell me all this yesterday?"

Starbuck wagged his head. "The game's not over till the last hand is dealt. I always like to have an ace up my sleeve."

"Judas Priest!" Bullock laughed and smote him across the back. "You're one of a kind, Luke! God-damn me if you're not!"

The driver let loose a leather-lunged shout. While the other passengers climbed aboard, the two men vigorously shook hands. There was a sense of celebration in their parting, and no maudlin words. Starbuck simply waved and stepped into the coach. Then he settled back in his seat with an inward sigh of relief.

He wasn't sorry to put Deadwood behind him.

Chapter Nineteen

Verna Phelps thought the article in poor taste. She adjusted her pince-nez and spread the Denver *Post* on her desk. A grisly account of the Deadwood killing was featured on the front page. Written with a certain ghoulish detail, the article pandered to the reading public's morbid sense of curiosity. She considered it a low form of yellow journalism.

Over the past week Starbuck had become a coast-to-coast news item. The story was first picked up by the *Police Gazette*, and quickly spread to papers all across the country. With bold headlines and purple prose, the tale of a detective who had killed both father and son was played as high drama. The seven-year lapse between killings, combined with the assassination plot, gave it an added degree of sensationalism. The furor in the nation's press served to enhance Starbuck's reputation, and his notoriety. He remained the most celebrated manhunter in the West.

The door opened and Verna glanced up from the paper. A fashionably dressed woman stepped into the office. She wore a tailored waistcoat, with an accordion-pleated skirt and a stylish hat decorated with an ostrich feather. She was slender, somewhere in her late forties, but well preserved and still very attractive. Verna folded the paper and nodded pleasantly.

"Good afternoon. May I help you?"

"Yes, please." The woman's voice was surprisingly genteel. "I wish to see Mr. Starbuck."

"Do you have an appointment?"

"I—" The woman smiled uncertainly. "I apologize, but I wasn't aware an appointment was necessary."

"May I inquire the nature of your visit?"

"A personal matter . . . confidential."

"I'm sorry," Verna said briskly. "Mr. Starbuck does not handle domestic cases. I suggest you try another agency."

"Oh, no!" The woman's lip trembled. "I assure you it has nothing to do with domestic difficulties. I wish to retain Mr. Starbuck on a business matter!"

"Perhaps you could provide me with the particulars?"

The woman averted her eyes. "I can only say it's a matter of the gravest importance. Anything else will have to be said to Mr. Starbuck personally."

"I see." Verna frowned, still not convinced. "May I ask your name?"

"Mrs. Roger Latham."

"Are you a resident of Denver, Mrs. Latham?"

"Yes, of course."

"Your current address?"

"Why do—" Mrs. Latham stopped, nervously clutching her purse. "It's 1038 Welton."

"Capitol Hill?"

Mrs. Latham inclined her head. "Quite near the governor's mansion."

"Please wait here."

Verna rose and moved to the door of Starbuck's office. She rapped lightly and entered, closing the door behind her. Several moments passed, the low murmur of voices audible from within the other room. Then the door opened and Verna reappeared.

"Won't you come in, Mrs. Latham." She motioned, stepping aside. "Mr. Starbuck will see you."

"Oh, thank you!"

The woman glided across the room and went past her. Starbuck was seated, his desk littered with an accumulation of correspondence. He stood, nodding to Verna, who quietly closed the door. Then he indicated a chair.

"Please be seated, Mrs. Latham."

"You're most kind, Mr. Starbuck. I do apologize for interrupting your busy schedule."

"No need." Starbuck waited until she took a chair before he sat down. "I was just clearing my desk. Nothing that won't wait."

Mrs. Latham looked at him fully for the first time. Her gaze was oddly clinical, almost an inspection. She smiled and shifted her purse to her lap.

"I must say you're not what I expected, Mr. Starbuck."

"Beg your pardon?"

"Well—" Her hand fluttered like a wounded bird. "A man in your profession conjures a certain image. I thought you would . . ."

Her voice trailed off, and Starbuck made an idle gesture. "No horns and no cloven hooves, Mrs. Latham. I do the Devil's work, but it ends there."

"Is that how you see it—the Devil's work?"

"A figure of speech," Starbuck said easily. "How

can I help you? I understand you're here on a matter of some importance."

"Yes, I am." A pulse throbbed in her neck. "I wish to retain your services."

"To what purpose?"

"A man stole something from me. Something very dear and very precious."

"You want me to run him down, reclaim your property?"

"No." Her mouth narrowed and her eyes took on the dull gleam of an icon. "I want him killed."

A sudden foreboding swept over Starbuck. He found himself unaccountably disquieted, every sense alert. He could see anger, resentment, and a trace of fear in her eyes. There was a strangeness about her—some haunting familiarity—and unbidden a tantalizing thought popped into his mind. He wondered on it a moment, almost let it slip away. Then he listened and heard again the last words of James Horn.

Kill me and you're a dead man for certain.

The woman across the desk watched him with utter directness. She was marvelously in control of herself, and yet there was something attenuated in her manner. She sat rigid, and a pinpoint of anguish lighted her gaze. He warned himself to proceed cautiously.

"How'd you happen to pick me?"

"You have no peer, Mr. Starbuck." She unsnapped the clasp on her purse, and took out a worn news clipping. "I realized that when I read of your last case."

Starbuck accepted the clipping. He scanned it quickly and saw that it dealt with the Deadwood killing. There was no byline and the dateline simply read

Dakota Territory. Yet the typeface was distinctive, unlike any he'd ever seen before. He casually placed the clipping on the desk.

"Offhand, I'd say that came from an eastern newspaper."

"Yes." Her voice dropped. "The New York *Morning Telegraph*."

"So you're not from Denver?"

"No."

"And you're not Mrs. Roger Latham?"

"No."

"Who are you, then?"

"Haven't you guessed?" She pulled a small pocket revolver from her purse. "I credited you with somewhat keener deductive powers, Mr. Starbuck."

"I'm generally quicker," Starbuck said lamely. "Course, the story I got was that you'd died some years back. I reckon Dutch Henry had his reasons for lying."

"Henry was a vain fool," she replied. "His pride wouldn't allow him to admit I divorced him."

"Or that you'd remarried?"

"Bravo!" she said without irony. "How clever of you, Mr. Starbuck."

"Only makes sense," Starbuck said, playing for time. "James was attending some eastern college when he got word his daddy had been killed. He came west to collect his inheritance and he never went back. The way that tallies out, he was trying to put something—or someone—behind him. I'd judge it wasn't you."

"No." Her expression was wistful, somehow vulnerable. "James loathed his stepfather almost as much as he loved Henry. The inheritance provided him with the wherewithal to start a new life . . . to escape."

"You must've missed him all those years?"

"Terribly," she admitted. "James and I were always very close. He wrote, of course, and whenever he came east on business, we always managed a visit. But it was never the same after Henry's death."

"I'm almost sorry I had to put Dutch Henry away."

"Regrets hardly seem in character for you, Mr. Starbuck."

"Not that, exactly." Starbuck feigned a hangdog look. "If I hadn't killed Dutch Henry, then you wouldn't have lost your son. See what I mean?"

"I bear you no grudge for Henry's death. He was scarcely a loss to mankind."

"The boy was, though," Starbuck added quickly. "Except for his daddy's influence, he would've turned out all right. Seemed like Dutch Henry had a hold on him—even from the grave."

"Are you trying to play on a mother's sympathy?"

"No, ma'am!" Starbuck protested. "I'm just saying life's not fair. Your son deserved better, a whole lot better!"

"Tell me, Mr. Starbuck"—her tone was raw with bitterness—"were those your thoughts the day you killed him?"

Starbuck slowly shook his head. "At the time, he was doing his level best to kill me."

"I read the newspaper articles."

"Then you know what I testified to at the coronor's inquest. He was mad for revenge, and he'd tried to have me assassinated several times. He wouldn't have stopped until I was dead."

"Do you honestly believe that matters?"

"I think it would if you gave it some thought."

"You killed my son!" She drew a deep, unsteady breath, and her voice rose quickly. "I gave that a great deal of thought, Mr. Starbuck! All the way from New York I thought of nothing else!"

"Ask yourself a question," Starbuck said gently. "What would you gain by killing me?"

"Please, Mr. Starbuck!" Her words were hard, contemptuous. "Don't beg pity! I have none left—none!"

"I'm not begging." Starbuck regarded her without guile. "I'm talking reason, common horse sense."

"Are you indeed?" she said stiffly, her lips white. "Very well, allow me to indulge you. What earthly reason would stop me from killing the man who killed my son?"

"You have too much to lose."

"Lose!" Her laugh was laced with scorn. "I have nothing left to lose. I've already lost it all—everything that matters!"

"A good look in a mirror might convince you otherwise."

"A mirror?"

"A look at yourself," Starbuck explained. "You're a cultured woman. You started out on a hard-scrabble farm—with an outlaw for a husband—and you've made yourself over into a lady. A real, honest-to-god lady! You shouldn't throw that away."

"Now you're attempting to play on my vanity!"

"Am I?" Starbuck asked softly. "You've got position and wealth, and a husband who thinks the world of you. I'd call that a plain fact, not vanity."

"How—" She seemed to falter, then rushed on. "How do you know those things?"

"A blind man could see it," Starbuck remarked. "The way you dress, the refined way you speak, all that says a lot about your husband. You must've told him about Dutch Henry—lies wouldn't have held up all these years—and he still married you, didn't he?"

She studied him a moment. "You should have been a lawyer, Mr. Starbuck. You plead a case very eloquently."

"It's your case, not mine. You shoot me and you're the big loser."

"I rather doubt that."

"Do you?" Starbuck said with genuine concern. "No matter how much you grieve your son, that'll pass. Some things you live with all your life. Killing a man in coldblood tops the list."

"The way you killed James?"

Starbuck sensed he'd lost. Her expression became immobile and her eyes glittered with hatred, naked and revealed. There was no remorse, no pity, in her look. A tightening around the mouth told him she was about to pull the trigger.

The door burst open. She was momentarily distracted, and in that split instant, Starbuck flung himself headlong to the floor. Then she fired; the slug drilled through the backrest of his chair and thunked into the wall. Her features twisted in a crazed look and she swiftly rose to her feet. She leaned across the desk.

"No!" Verna cried from the doorway. *"Don't!"*

She ignored the command. Bracing herself against the desk, she thrust out her arm and pointed the revolver at Starbuck. Her hand shook violently as her finger curled tighter around the trigger. Verna took dead aim with a double-barrel derringer and shot her in the leg. Her mouth froze in a silent oval, then the revolver barked and a bullet whizzed past Starbuck's head. She stared at him a moment, and suddenly the light went out in her eyes. Her legs collapsed and the gun dropped from her hand. She slowly folded to the floor.

Starbuck stood and moved around the desk. He looked first at the woman, then his gaze shuttled to the doorway. Verna appeared steady, not in the least shocked by what she'd done. He shook his head in open wonder.

"Where'd you get the derringer?"

"Out of my pocketbook."

"I never figured you to carry a gun."

Verna sniffed. "You never bothered to ask. As it happens, I am an expert markswoman."

"Lucky for me you are," Starbuck said gratefully. "How'd you know she wasn't on the level?"

"The address," Verna observed. "She told me she lived at 1038 Welton. I checked it in the city street directory. Welton ends at the 800 block."

"Loose ends," Starbuck said absently, staring at the woman. "Guess you'd better run fetch a doctor. No sense letting her bleed to death."

"Oh?" Verna looked surprised. "I do believe there's hope for you yet!"

"How so?"

"Perhaps you're not the cynic you think."

"Whatever I am"—Starbuck's mouth lifted in an ashen grin—"you're a sweetheart. I wouldn't trade you for all the tea in China!"

Verna flushed and tittered a giddy laugh. She

turned quickly away, pausing only long enough to
drop the derringer on her desk. Then she hurried out
the door.

Still chuckling to himself, Starbuck knelt beside
the fallen woman. He took her wrist between thumb
and forefinger; her pulse was strong and her color
appeared good. On the verge of rising, his attention
was drawn to her purse. He opened it and pawed
through the contents. A brief search turned up a
silver-filigreed calling-card case. He recognized it as
the type commonly carried by society ladies and
wealthy matrons. He extracted an embossed card and
read it with mild shock.

Her name was Mrs. Cornelius Vanderbilt II.

A gentle breeze drifted through the window. The bedroom was dark, lighted only by the dim glow of a
lamp from the sitting room. Lola lay quietly in the
crook of his arm, her head pillowed on his shoulder.
She was satiated, drifting on the tranquil flame of
their lovemaking. Yet she was wide awake, and
thoughtful.

Earlier, he'd told her about the shooting. Verna's
part was related in some detail, and she had emerged
the heroine of the piece. All else, including his conversation with Horn's mother, had been somewhat
fuzzy in the telling. Oddly, he'd skipped over several
salient points, leapfrogging from the shooting to the
bare bones of the aftermath. The woman had been
taken to the hospital, and a full recovery was expected. The particulars, all the savory little tidbits, had
been bypassed. He'd simply stopped there, and said
no more.

At the time, Lola had curbed her curiosity. But

now, with her imagination running wild, she could restrain herself no longer. She snuggled closer, her breath warm and velvety against his ear.

"Lover?"

"Hmmm?"

"What will happen to her . . . Horn's mother?"

"Nothing."

"Nothing!" Lola pushed up on one elbow. "Aren't you going to press charges?"

"Nope."

"Why not?" Lola demanded. "She tried to kill you!"

"Happens all the time."

"Very funny! What happens when she tries again? You know she'll try!"

"I got a hunch that says she won't."

"Ooo God! It's like pulling teeth! What kind of hunch?"

"Well—" Starbuck nibbled her nipple, grinned. "I reckon she's got it out of her system now. We had a long talk at the hospital, and I'm satisfied bygones are bygones. She agreed to leave town the minute the doctors give her the okay."

"Where will she go?"

"Beats me."

"What name does she go by?"

"Mizz Horn," Starbuck said dreamily. "What else?"

"Some detective!" Lola lifted an eyebrow, studied him with mock seriousness. "What you need is a keeper. Or better yet—a bodyguard!"

"No," Starbuck said, nuzzling her breast. "All I need's a body!"

"Any old body?" Lola inquired with a naughty wink. "Or somebody special?"

"What do you think?"

Lola's laugh was a delicious sound. "I think I'm all the body you can handle, Mr. Starbuck!"

"Do you, now?"

"You don't believe me?"

"Let's just say I'm willing to be convinced."

"How long do I have?"

"All the time it takes."

"Braggart!" Lola darted his ear with her tongue. "You won't last that long!"

"Try me and see."

The moon went down over Denver before they were finished. She fell away limp and exhausted, but secretly pleased with herself. However far he roamed, even when he strayed, she knew he would never forget tonight. She'd spoiled him for other women, and the memory would linger. A bright ember, quickly fanned to flame, and always there. His bed was hers.

Starbuck slept the sleep of the weary warrior. He dreamed not of ghosts but of people. He held her close and thought no more of death.

Epilogue

Telluride, Colorado
June 24, 1889

"**H**ow many were in the gang?"

"Seven or eight." The express messenger sounded doubtful. "I didn't exactly have time to count noses."

Starbuck nodded. "Your report to the main office said the holdup took place outside Placerville?"

"You familiar with the valley?"

"Not all that much."

"Well, there's a bridge that crosses the San Miguel. I'd put it maybe five miles this side of Placerville. That's where they hit us."

"How'd they stop the train?"

"It was in my report," the messenger said testily. "They dropped a rock slide across the tracks."

"Just checking," Starbuck replied casually. "How about a description? Anything special you remember?"

"I damn sure remember the one that gave the orders! He kept a gun in my ear the whole god-blessed time!"

"What'd he look like?"

"Your size, maybe a little taller. Had black hair

and a mustache, and chewed tobacco. Sonovabitch spit like a grasshopper!"

"Hear any names?"

"Not that I recollect."

The train whistle tooted three sharp blasts. Starbuck hastily concluded the interrogation. He had all the information he needed, and he saw no reason to delay departure. After shaking hands, the messenger hoisted himself into the express car. The engine chuffed a cloud of steam and the driving wheels spun, slowly took purchase on the tracks. A few moments later the train pulled away from the platform.

Starbuck turned and walked past the stationhouse. On his way uptown, he mentally reviewed all he'd learned. The description fitted a known train robber, Charlie Stroud. Operating out of Robbers Roost, Stroud led a gang whose numbers varied according to the job. His territory extended south into New Mexico and Arizona, and he had pulled a string of holdups over the last year. He was elusive and a good tactician; running him to ground would be no easy task. Robbers Roost was as inhospitable as ever, still a hazardous undertaking for any lawman. Which made it even more so for a detective.

By now the trail was cold. The train had been robbed almost a week ago, and the gang had made off with some thirty thousand dollars in loot. Hired to run them down, Starbuck had arrived in Telluride only last night. The town was located in southern Colorado, on the western slope of the Rockies. Overlooking the San Miguel Valley, it was one of the newer mining camps, with a railroad spur and a thriving business community. To the northwest, some two hundred miles distant, lay Robbers Roost.

Starbuck judged it to be a four- or five-day ride. Adding another week or so to make contact with the outlaws, that would allow time for him to sprout a scruffy beard. From his valise, which he'd left in the hotel, he would select whatever else was needed to complete his disguise. All that remained was to buy a horse and pick up a used saddle. He turned onto Main Street and went looking for a stable. A block ahead he spotted Searle's Livery.

As he approached the stable, he saw three men push through the bat-wing doors of a nearby saloon. They stopped, huddling on the boardwalk in conversation. He automatically checked out the two men facing him, but neither of them was familiar. The third man, whose back was to him, appeared to be doing most of the talking. He dismissed them from mind and angled off toward the livery. Then the third man turned sideways, gesturing obliquely across the street. His features were distinct in the bright morning sun.

Thunderstruck, Starbuck halted dead in his tracks. Almost seven years had passed since they'd last met. The lithe frame was taller now, heavier and padded with muscle. The face was older, somewhere in the early twenties, visibly toughened by time. Yet there was no mistaking the broad brow and the square jaw, and the quick youthful look of a jester. The man doing the talking was Butch Cassidy.

Abruptly, the conversation ended. Butch dismissed the other men with a gesture, and they hurried down the boardwalk. Starbuck got himself untracked, walking toward them at a leisurely pace. He passed them as they turned into the dim interior of the stable. Proceeding upstreet, he stepped onto the boardwalk and strolled toward the saloon. Butch was still turned away, lost in thought. Starbuck followed the direction of his gaze and grunted softly to himself. Across the street, catty-corner to the saloon, was the San Miguel Valley Bank.

"Hello, Butch." He stopped a pace away. "How's tricks?"

Butch jumped, then whirled around. His jaw dropped open and his features corkscrewed in a look of doglike amazement. His eyes were veined with disbelief.

"I'll be go to hell!" he croaked. "Luke Starbuck!"

"In the flesh."

"Where'd you come from?"

"The depot." Starbuck jerked a thumb over his shoulder. "Passed your friends, and saw you standing here big as life."

"Couple of my drinkin' buddies," Butch said with an uneasy smile. "What brings you to Telluride?"

"Train robbers," Starbuck remarked. "Somebody pulled a holdup down around Placerville last week."

"No kiddin'?" Butch inquired innocently. "You still in the detective business, are you?"

"Only trade I know," Starbuck commented. "How about you? You're a long way from Hole-in-the-Wall."

"Yeah, I called it quits up there almost four years back."

"Where do you call home these days?"

"I drift around . . . nowhere special."

Starbuck's look betrayed nothing. "Whatever happened to Mike Cassidy?"

"You won't believe it!" Butch laughed, and for a moment there was a vestige of the clownish youngster in his features. "That old scutter done up and quit the owlhoot! Last I heard, he'd settled down somewheres south of the border. Got himself a señorita and a whole passel of kids!"

"Good for him," Starbuck said warmly. "How long ago was it he quit?"

"Summer of '85." Butch's expression turned sober. "That's when I packed it in at Hole-in-the-Wall. Wouldn't never've been the same, not without Mike."

"So you've been drifting around ever since?"

"More or less."

Starbuck sensed a sudden tension. Butch's gaze went past him, and he turned his head slightly. Out of the corner of his eye, he saw the other two men cross the street, leading three saddled horses. They glanced toward the saloon, and Butch nodded with an almost imperceptible movement. Then they continued on to the hitch rack outside the bank. After the horses were tied, one of the men stooped down and pretended to check the cinch on his mount. The other man took up a post near the bank entrance.

"Mike had the right idea," Starbuck said evenly. "You ought to try it yourself."

"Well, like I told you once, life's too goddang daily. A fellow stands still and before you know it, he takes root."

"Is that why you aim to rob the bank?"

Butch gave him a lightning frown. "Stay out of it, Luke! It's none of your concern!"

"Wish it weren't," Starbuck said in a low voice. "But here in Colorado, I'm sworn to uphold the law. I'd have to stop you."

"You'll die tryin'!" Butch ducked his chin toward the bank. "Those boys are meaner'n bitch wolves.

You stick your nose where it don't belong and they'll kill you dead!"

"I'd still be obliged to try."

"Christ on a crutch!" Butch grimaced, darted a quick look around. "Awright, lemme level with you, Luke. We've got the town marshal in our hip pocket! Bought him for a share of the pie and a promise he'd make himself scarce while we pulled the job. Now, you just stop and think about it! If the local lawdog don't care—why the hell should you?"

Starbuck regarded him with a cool look of appraisal. "Even if it's true, it doesn't change things. I'm here and I'd be bound to stop you."

"Goddamnit, you owe me!" Butch muttered fiercely. "I could've shot you that time at Hole-in-the-Wall! I had you dead to rights and all I did was crack your skull. You know you owe me, Luke!"

Starbuck looked him straight in the eye. "You're sure you want to call the marker that way?"

"You damn betcha I'm sure!"

"Then you've got yourself a deal, Butch."

"Well, now, I always knew you was a man that paid your debts!"

"One last condition," Starbuck said tightly. "You kill anyone and I'll drop you the minute you walk out of that bank."

"Fair enough!" Butch crowed. "I ain't never killed nobody in my life. I don't aim to start now!"

"We're even, then." Starbuck's voice was edged. "Next time all bets are off."

"What makes you think there'll be a next time?"

"Sooner or later somebody will want your ticket punched."

"And they'll call on you to do the job . . . that it?"

Starbuck's mouth set in a hard line. "Let's just say I'm the chief ticket-puncher hereabouts."

Butch began a question, then appeared to change his mind. He shrugged and turned away, mumbling as he walked off. "See you, Luke."

"Hope you don't and wish you're right."

There was no reply. Butch crossed the street without looking back. He nodded to the man at the hitch rack, whose assignment was to guard the horses and warn passersby away. Then he mounted the boardwalk and joined the man at the door. Together, they entered the bank. A moment later the door closed and the blind was drawn.

Starbuck moved back into the shade. He leaned against the wall of the saloon and took his time lighting a cigarette. Over the years, he'd wondered about Butch, recalling their train ride from Pueblo. The youngster had turned him down then—refusing a chance to go straight—and things clearly hadn't changed. The only difference was that Butch had now raised his sights. He had himself a gang and he felt cocky enough to tackle a bank. Still, for all his bravado, it was apparently his first try at the big time. Starbuck had heard nothing of him on the grapevine, and there were no wanted posters bearing his name. For seven years, he'd been a cipher among western outlaws. Today, all that went by the boards.

Old memories flooded back in a rush. Starbuck tried to remember the last time he'd thought of Hole-in-the-Wall and Deadwood. And James Horn. As near as he could recall, it was sometime the spring of '84. He'd received a letter from Seth Bullock, advising him a grand jury had finally returned an indictment against Governor Nehemiah Ordway. That it had

taken Bullock two years to secure an indictment
merely underscored Ordway's political power in Dakota Territory. The outcome of the trial, held that
summer, bordered on travesty. Ordway's lawyer entered a motion to quash the indictment; the brief con-
tended that a territorial governor, appointed by the
president, was not subject to the jurisdiction of a territorial court. The judge granted the motion, and all
charges were dismissed. No effort was made to secure
an indictment by a federal grand jury.

Starbuck was scarcely surprised by subsequent
events. Less than two weeks after the trial, President
Chester Arthur removed Ordway from office. While
hardly a whitewash, the president's action nonetheless
ended any hope of criminal prosecution. Ordway,
with no fear for the future, devoted himself to a business empire founded on the graft and bribes he'd accepted while governor. Nor was he tarred and
feathered in the political arena; his reputation was still
intact, and his influence on the Potomac suffered none
at all. The Northern Pacific Railroad hired him as a
lobbyist, and a good part of his time thereafter was
spent in Washington. He emerged a man of wealth
and prominence, and in the process he disproved the
old axiom about crime. He'd made it pay.

Once more, Starbuck's cynicism regarding politicians had withstood the test. There was no justice
for those who held membership in the Order of
Strange Bedfellows. His investigation, all the evidence of graft and corruption, had proved little more
than an exercise in futility. His time in Deadwood had
produced only one tangible result. He'd killed a man
who deserved to die. In retrospect, he saw that summary justice was the only lasting justice. He thought

it a sad commentary on life, and yet it was enough for him. He still lived, and James Horn was dead.

His reverie into the past abruptly ended. The bank door opened and Butch stepped outside. He was trailed by his cohort, who carried a gunnysack stuffed with cash. Their guns were drawn and they walked directly to the hitch rack. Along the street, several townspeople gawked a moment in disbelief, then quickly scattered for cover. Butch and the other men stepped into the saddle and reined their horses away from the bank. No cry of alarm was raised and no one attempted to stop them. All of Telluride seemed to hold its breath.

Starbuck moved from the shade into the sunlight. He took a final drag on his cigarette and ground it underfoot as the robbers neared the corner. Butch glanced in his direction, and for an instant their eyes locked. An unspoken message passed between them, and in that fragmented moment the youngster's face looked somehow like a sad clown. Then he laughed and gigged his horse.

With Butch in the lead, the robbers rounded the corner. They spurred their mounts into a gallop and rode north out of town. Yipping and howling, they aimed their sixguns skyward and blasted off several rounds. The getaway was loud and noisy, somehow amateurish, and almost comic to watch. They were like exuberant schoolboys, filled with their own devilment, tossing lighted strings of firecrackers into the air. Their horses abreast, they pounded out of Telluride in a cloud of dust. A short stretch down the road they vanished from sight.

Starbuck took the pragmatic view. The kid had called the marker and their account was now settled.

Yet he saw today as a beginning, not an end.

Butch Cassidy was wild as the wind, bound and determined to live unfettered by rules. The Telluride bank robbery truly branded him an outlaw, and he possessed all the attributes of the breed. One day his picture would appear on wanted posters and a price would be put on his head. Then an angry banker or a railroad baron would issue a summary death warrant. From that moment onward, the youngster would be living on borrowed time.

Starbuck turned and walked toward the livery stable. He had a train robber to catch, and the first order of business was to get himself aboard a horse. Still, for all that, there was no escaping his own vision of the future. When the time finally rolled around, he somehow knew he was the one who would be summoned. It was in the cards, ordained by the caprice that governed such things. He would be assigned the job of killing Butch Cassidy.

He promised himself to do it swiftly.

America's Authentic Voice of the Western Frontier

Matt Braun
Bestselling author of *Bloody Hand*

HICKOK & CODY

In the wind-swept campsite of the Fifth Cavalry Regiment, along Red Willow Creek, Russia's Grand Duke Alexis has arrived to experience the thrill of the buffalo hunt. His guides are: Wild Bill Hickok and Buffalo Bill Cody—two heroic dead-shots with a natural flair for showmanship, a hunger for adventure, and the fervent desire to keep the myths of the Old West alive. But what approached from the East was a journey that crossed the line into dangerous territory. It would offer Alexis a front row seat to history, and would set Hickok and Cody on a path to glory.

"Braun tackles the big men, the complex personalities of those brave few who were pivotal figures in the settling of an untamed frontier."
—Jory Sherman, author of *Grass Kingdom*

"Matt Braun has a genius for taking real characters out of the Old West and giving them flesh-and-blood immediacy."
—Dee Brown, author of *Bury My Heart at Wounded Knee*

AVAILABLE WHEREVER BOOKS ARE SOLD
FROM ST. MARTIN'S PAPERBACKS

HC 8/02

AMERICA'S AUTHENTIC VOICE OF THE WESTERN FRONTIER

Matt Braun
BESTSELLING AUTHOR OF *HICKOK & CODY*

THE WILD ONES

Into the West of the 1870s came a family of New York City stage performers: a widowed father, his son, and a daughter whose beauty and singing voice could make the most hardened frontiersmen weep. The Fontaine family was not prepared for the life they found across the Mississippi. From Abilene to Dodge City, they crossed paths with some of the legendary figures on the frontier, from Jesse James to Bill Hickok and General George Custer. All the while, the Fontaines kept searching for a place to settle down— until they set their sights on the boomtown called Denver. Awaiting Lillian Fontaine in Denver are fame and loss, fortune and betrayal. But between Dodge and her destiny are a thousand miles of unconquered country, an outlaw band, and one man who will force the young songstress to give the performance of her life . . .

"Matt Braun is a master storyteller of frontier fiction."

—Elmer Kelton

"Matt Braun is head and shoulders above all the rest who would attempt to bring the gunmen of the Old West to life."

—Terry C. Johnston, author of
The Plainsmen series

**AVAILABLE WHEREVER BOOKS ARE SOLD
FROM ST. MARTIN'S PAPERBACKS**

WO 8/02